The Quest for Earthly Delights

The Chronicles of Datch

By David Hallam

ISBN: 978-1-917238-17-5

DEDICATION

3

For Emma.

ACKNOWLEDGMENTS

I want to say thank you to all the staff in my local public house for putting up with me sitting in the corner typing away on my laptop.

I would also like to thank my proof readers for all their help with proof reading. It is a very large challenge for them as my spelling and grammar are about as solid as a glass of milkshake.

Honeymoon

Datch lives on Bellatrix Five and is a successful rock star. He has his own starship called the Raven which he and his band The Pack use for galactic tours. Datch along with his friends have a knack for helping people and have already saved one president and two planetary systems. They are not only rock stars but also have become ambassadors and spiritual leaders for Welly four. This involved a lot of partying which is another thing The Pack are good at. Datch has just become joined to his long-term girlfriend Carina at a very posh event in Traxsent on the Planet of Bellatrix Five. During the ceremony Datch and Carina were telepathically joined by the monks from Welly four. The link only works when their rings are energised and that is done by partying.

Now it's honeymoon time.

Datch and Carina sat in the cockpit looking at the stars. The Raven had just cleared Bellatrixian orbit and was heading into clear space.

"So, which one babes?" Asked Datch.

"Let's find one with a quiet beach somewhere."

"What about Luyten seven. That is quite a lazy planet and has got that nice beach resort we went to a couple of years ago."

"Ok, then we can work out where to go from there."

"Computer set course for Luyten seven, interspace seventeen. Standard alarm."

"Course laid in. Journey time will be eighteen hours."

"Engage."

The Raven turned on its own axis and then the stars out of the window winked out and started to flicker.

"So, what do you want to do for eighteen hours?" Asked Datch.

Carina stood up, looked at him and smiled.

"Oh, that." He said grinning.

They headed out of the cockpit in the direction of the bedroom.

Seventeen hours later the Raven's alarm sounded. Datch and Carina were in the cargo bay playing a one-on-one game of Solar Ball. They finished the game and headed up to the cockpit and sat down. Datch picked up his head set and put it on.

"Luyten Control, this is Starship Raven on approach to Luyten seven."

"Good afternoon, Raven, Traffic is light at the moment please lock onto beacon 719 for orbital approach. Please Transmit your IDs and manifest."

Datch pressed some virtual buttons.

"Thank you, Raven. Just the two of you? No cargo?"

"No Cargo and yes, just the two of us. We're on honeymoon."

"Congratulations and welcome to Luyten.

"Luyten Control, requesting beacon for Tarasands resort complex."

"Raven change to beacon TRS771 on orbital interface."

"Thanks, Luyten control. Raven out."

In the centre of the flickering stars outside a bright spec appeared and started to get larger. Then as the bright sphere half filled the view and lights dimmed as the Raven dropped out of interspace. There in front of them was a planet with glittering blue oceans across its equator and above it white fluffy clouds floated in the sky. In the northern hemisphere a large storm system was at work and they could see the lightning flashing across the cloud tops. Datch entered orbit and then locked the Raven onto the beacon for the resort.

"Luyten control, this is the Raven. We are commencing planet fall. Locked onto resorts beacon."

"OK Raven. Enjoy your stay. Please contact Tarasands for final approach."

"Thank you Luyten control. Raven out."

The Raven dived down towards the planet's surface. Below the ocean waves got larger as they descended. Datch levelled the Raven out at four thousand metres and headed for the coast. Ten minutes later they were walking down the ramp at the back of the Raven with their swim wear on. They stopped at the bottom of the ramp where an attendant was waiting for them.

"Welcome sir and mam."

"Thank you," said Datch.

"Do you require any services while you're here?"

"Yes Please. Can you refuel the Raven for us."

"Certainly sir. Is there anything else you require?"

"No, that's it thanks."

"In which case sir, you can find the main resort over there through the gate. Also, if you require anything please do not hesitate to ask a member of staff."

"Thanks again."

With that Datch and Carina headed over to the gate.

The resort had a private beach which was a light pink colour due to the rocks in the local geology and had palm trees along the shore. Behind the beach were a number of pools also surrounded with palm trees and a number of bars dotted about. At the back of the resort was the main restaurant with the gate to the landing area. Also, Behind the landing area were a number of small villas for people who didn't wish to stay on their ships.

Datch and Carina were scanned at the gate and were allowed to go in. They headed over to a couple of sunbeds at the top of the beach and sat down. Moments later a waiter appeared.

"Welcome to Tarasands resort. Could I get you both a drink?"

"Sure, I'll have a beer and..." Datch looked at Carina. "My wife will have a Traxsent starburst please."

"Thank you, sir. Do you require any food?"

"Not at the moment, Thank you."

"Thank you, sir. I'll just go and fetch your drinks for you."

Datch settled down on the sunbed and a voice in his head said '*It's nice here, isn't it?*'

He then answered it.

'*Yes, and I love the pink sand.*'

'*So, have you had any thoughts about where we are going?*'

'*No, not really. But did you know the Sol star system is not far from here?*'

'That's where your dad got the Ice cream from, isn't it?'

'Yes, maybe we could nip over and get some of the proper stuff to compare it.'

'Err, they haven't made contact yet.'

'I know, we would have to sneak in, go to an Ice cream parlour for ice-cream and take off again without anyone knowing.'

Just then the waiter came back with the drinks.

"Here you are sir, one beer for you and a Traxsent Starburst for mam."

"Thank you." said Datch.

"Yes. thanks." Added Carina.

"Can I get you anything else?"

"Err, do you have any ice cream?"

"We have Chocolate and Renar berry sir."

"Err, can we have two helpings of Chocolate please?"

"Certainly sir."

With that the waiter headed off between the palm trees, Datch turned to look at Carina.

"So, what do you think. You did want an adventure?"

"Well, ok. It sounds like fun. How primitive are they?"

Datch looked into space for a few moments while he accessed his implant.

"The last survey was two years ago. It said that they were still using radio wave detection systems, they have rocket propulsion and a very basic low power Ion drive. The population arrange from primitive bush people to level 3 on intelligence scale. Most races are friendly enough but can still be war like and aggressive towards each other."

"Ok. What level are we? And can we sneak in without them seeing us?"

"We're are at intelligence level 342 and yes, the scattering field on the Raven will make it invisible to them. We just need to find somewhere to park her out the way."

"Ok then, an ice cream hunt it is."

The waiter came back with two bowls filled with ice cream.

"Thank you." they said and started eating the ice cream.

"So," said Datch after the waiter had gone, "when do you want to go?"

"Well, let's have a couple of days here and then head there. How far is it."

Datch looked into space again for a moment.

"12.5 light years, so about two hours."

"Cool."

"I've brought a couple of orbital interspace transceivers so we can keep a connection for our implants. It might be a little slow because the nearest interstellar node is about a light year away so the interspace link will be quite small reducing the bandwidth."

"Well, it will add to the adventure. What about the language?"

"Well, they seem to have a lot of them and virtually all are not in the galactic database. The only one it has matrixes for is one that they have classed as the international language. It's called English."

"Oh, what a boring name."

"Yes, but if we upload it, we should be able to speak it quite easily."

They both then had a look concentration on their faces.

"So, how do I sound?" said Datch in English.

"Oh, very good, squire." Said Carina.

They both burst out laughing.

"Oh, look, it's got different dialects. How about this one." Datch screwed his face up and then said.

"Hello Sheela, chuck another steak on the barbi." In an Australian accent.

"What about this one." added Carina before saying.

"There's lobsters on the south beach Datch." in and Jamaican accent.

They both laughed again.

"OK, we had better download all the accents so we can fit in."

"Good Plan."

It took a few minutes to go through all the dialects but finally they were all stored.

"Shall we go for a swim?"

"Yes, my dear. After you." replied Carina in a posh British accent.

They headed down to the beach and into the sea for a splash about and a swim.

The next day they went shopping for adventuring supplies and found a shop selling off grid supplies for the adventure tourist.

Inside it had tents, camping equipment, various distress beacons, scanning equipment, medical kits and clothing. They stood looking at the medical supplies.

"Do we need any of these?" asked Carina.

"Grab a small kit, dad gave me a box of military grade nanobots for any big emergencies. He said 'knowing me, we would likely need them'. There is also a full emergency kit onboard the Raven, so, we just need things for bites and minor mishaps while we're out and about."

"Well, if we get one of these and that one as well?" said Carina picking a pink box.

"Ok, I'll get a planetary distress beacon. We'll link it to the Raven's systems so if the Raven picks it up, she will send an interstellar distress signal."

"What about food packs?"

"Yes, might be an idea. You do that and I'll get the beacon."

Carina went over to the food rack and got a selection of different foods. Then she collected a couple of food heaters before heading off to find Datch. He was looking at the guns.

"Do we need them?"

"Yes, I was looking at all the information on Sol three. It does have a number of animal lifeforms that would see us as lunch."

"Oh. You will have to teach me to shoot."

"They have a range out the back and the sign says they can give you lessons."

"Ok, can we do that?"

"Yes, what gun would you like?"

They stood looking at the weapons. Datch selected a large hunting rifle and plasma pistol that he could keep next to him, he also got a portable defence screen to stop any unwelcome visitors at night. Carina went for the same pistol and also got a slightly smaller rifle that she thought would suit her.

They headed over to the counter with a large trolly full of bits.

"Hello," said the cashier, "Looks like you're ready to invade a planet." She joked.

"Well, this our first trip into the wilderness," said Datch.

"Yes, and can we have a shooting lesson please?" Added Carina.

"It looks like you're well prepared and yes, let me complete the sale and I'll call Pete over and he'll take you out back with your weapons." The cashier said as she scanned two large hunting knives and a plasma stick.

"How much is the lesson?"

"As you have bought the guns today the first one is free, but if you need a second it will be twenty credits each."

"Ok Thanks."

The cashier finished putting the items through the scanner.

"Would you like them packed up?" She asked.

"Yes please, apart from the guns."

"Ok, that will be one thousand, two hundred and fifty-seven credits please."

Datch looked at the till and a box appeared in his mind.

He clicked the virtual box and the till beeped.

"Thank you, Sir. One moment please."

She pressed a button on the till.

"Pete, please come to the front desk."

She turned back to them.

"He'll be here in a moment. I'll send the rest of your item to be stored in box 7, you'll be able to collect them on the way out."

"Ok, thanks." said Datch picking up his pistol and rifle. Carina did the same.

A few moments later a man came walking over.

"This is Pete, he'll take you through the gun training."

"Hello." He said walking up and shaking their hands.

"Is this the first time you have handled weapons."

"I have done a little bit of training with the IPSF but Carina hasn't had any."

"Ok, no problem. Just follow me please."

They were taken into the back of the shop and down a corridor. They went through the door at the end and into a large room with holo projectors set up at the far end and the far wall was protected by a force field.

"Right folks, let's try the rifles first. If you could both take them out of their covers I'll run through the workings of them."

Datch and Carina took the rifles out. Pete walked over to Carina.

"Carina, is that right?"

"Yes."

"OK, Carina. This is the target sight, this is the safety lock, this here is the main power pack, and this is the trigger. This bit here is the butt, place it against your shoulder like so."

He helped her place the butt against her right shoulder and made sure her hands were in the right place.

"Ok, you just try lifting it up and down a few times until you find it comfortable while I go through it with Datch."

"Yes sir." said Carina, Datch nodded.

"Ok, Datch. Were you watching me go through it with Carina?"

"Yes, Sir."

"Ok then, show me which bits are which."

Datch went through pointing out all the bits as well as a couple of extra bits.

"So, you have used a gun before?" Asked Pete.

"Well, I was shown how to use one last year but never needed to fire it."

"Ok, in which case let's see how you handle it."

Datch picked it up and placed it against his shoulder looking down the range.

"Good. Carina are you ok?"

"Yes." she said.

"Right let's see how you can shoot."

He picked up a vid com off the counter in front of him and pressed a couple of buttons. At the end of the room two large holographic targets appeared with a scoreboard above them.

"Ok, press the power button."

There were two subtle clicks followed by the noise of plasma being charged.

"Good, now point the rifles at the target and release the safety switch."

Datch looked through the target sight and took aim at the target.

"Now be prepared for a bit of a kick in your shoulder and make sure you relax. Ok, when you're ready take a shot."

Datch slowly pressed the fire button. All of a sudden there was a thud from the rifle and it kicked back into his shoulder. at the same time a bolt of plasma shot down the range hitting the outer ring of the target. Then Datch heard Carina's gun fire and a little gasp from her. She also hit the outer ring.

"Hey, not bad folks, not bad at all. Ok, to make this fun, let's see who can get the best out of ten. Let me just reset the targets."

He pressed a button and the targets cleared. This time they had numbers in them and a score counter above them lit up.

Datch looked at Carina and she nodded.

What happened next was a bit like the shootout at the O K corral. Plasma bolt after plasma bolt shot down the range. Finally, they both had their ten shots.

"OK? I can see you're both quite happy at using the rifles." he said looking down the range at the smoking holes in the targets.

"Carina, it looks like you beat Datch by one point."

"Do I get a bonus point for shooting the scoreboard?" Asked Datch.

Pete looked and sure enough there was a hole through the middle of the zero with smoke coming out of it.

"Err, no, sorry. Ok, moving on. I take you are planning to use these for hunting?"

"Yes, if we need to."

"Ok, Let's put up some game creatures."

He pressed a few buttons on vid and the range turned into a woodland scene. A deer was standing in the centre and was currently frozen in place.

"Right. In order to kill the deer, you will need to hit it in the head. This is so the animal does not suffer and death is instantaneous. The last thing you want is the animal to be wounded and suffer a long death if you can't find it. You can also shoot it in the heart, that will kill it within a few seconds as well. So, for the head shot aim for here."

He pressed another button and a red circle appeared on the deer's head

"And here for the heart."

Another red circle appeared on its rib cage.

"Ok Carina, take a shot at its head."

Carina fired and took its ear off.

The deer didn't look happy.

"Close, Try again."

She did and put a hole through its head.

"Good, that's better, Datch you're up." he said and reset the deer.

Datch took his first shot and took its nose off.

"Well at least it won't smell you coming anymore. Try again."

Datch did and hit it between the eyes.

"Good, let's see how you get on with a live target."

He pressed a few buttons and the deer vanished. A lot more plants appeared and then amongst the foliage deer could be seen grazing on some leaves.

"Ok, the deer are going to be moving around, take your time and take the head shot. Carina, you go for the ones on the right and Datch, you take the ones on the left."

They started shooting, the deer looked unimpressed. One lost an ear, another a leg and one ended up missing a tail.

"Ok, you're both tensing up. Relax and let it happen."

They both let out a sigh and relaxed a bit.

They started shooting again. This time they started getting kill shots. Pete slowly increased the level of hardness. After twenty minutes they were hitting the deer most of the time and a lot of the hits were kill shots.

"Ok, folks, I think you've got the rifles now. Let me show you how to charge your power packs before you put them away. Then we'll move onto pistol training."

Pete showed them how to remove the power packs and how to use the chargers. Then it was time for the pistols.

"I take it you've got these for personal protection?"

"Yes, just in case of wild animals. We have a defence shield to put up at night but you never know what's going to happen during the day," said Datch and Carina nodded.

"Ok, in which case we will run this program." He pressed a few buttons and a jungle scene appeared.

"Right, if you want to follow me."

They headed around the counter.

"Please put these on. They are personal shields and will stop any stray rounds from hurting us."

They clipped the little boxes onto their waists and pressed the little button. A shield lit up around them before going invisible.

"Oh wow, this is quite cool. Do you sell them?" asked Datch.

"Yes, we do."

"Oh cool, can we buy four of them please. We might need spares."

"Yes, and judging by the last round in the jungle you may need them."

Pete paused for a moment, and then continued.

"Right, various creatures are going to come out of the jungle at you, keep your safeties off and be ready to shoot. The pistols do have a small kick back but you can hold them with one hand quite easily. OK, turn the safeties off, here we go."

Datch and Carina got their pistols out and made them ready. Pete pressed a couple of buttons on his vid com.

A creature appeared near Carina ready to pounce on her. Both Datch and Carina turned together and fired at the same time both shots sent the creature to oblivion.

"Wow, nice shooting."

Another creature appeared next to Datch and met the same fate. Then another and another, each time both Datch and Carina would fire at same time and it would be a kill shot. Pete increased the level again and again. Each time they would fire together and each time the creature would die. After twenty minutes of watching Datch and Carina kill everything the computer could throw at them Pete stopped it.

"Ok folks, I've seen some things in my time but you two are something else. You shoot together, turn together, hell you even have the same expressions on you faces. So, what's the crack, you just beat the computer!"

Datch turned to Pete,

"Err, we sort of have a telepathic link. So, I see her thoughts,"

"and, I see his," finished Carina.

"Oh boy. And you have guns. Well, God help anything that comes up on you two."

Datch grinned and so did Carina. Pete wondered if he was going to see them on the news channel later.

"You're not planning any planetary invasions, are you?"

"No, we're just going for ice-cream." said Datch and smiled.

"Oh, ok, well judging by the fact the computer could not hit you, I think you're good to go."

"Cool, do you think we should get extra power packs?" asked Carina.

"Yes, it's always handy to have a spare one just in case."

"OK, can we have two for each weapon please?"

"Sure, no problem."

"Err," said Datch, "Is there any way I can link this to our ships weapon systems?"

"Why?" Said Pete, now slightly worried.

"Well, if we are being say chased by a lot of enraged deer and we have to run towards the ship then I was thinking that it may be handy to have the ships pulse canons available. That way we can lay down covering fire while we get on board."

"Well, I don't know about enraged deer, But I see your point. You're defiantly not planning on invading any planets, are you?"

"No." said Carina now giving him the puppy dog eyes.

"Ok, yes we sell trackers in the store." He said starting to weaken under Carina's onslaught.

"Cool, can I have two please?" asked Datch.

"Yes, please." added Carina smiling.

"I'll get them for you on the way out. Ok, Power down your weapons and put them in their holders please."

They did and then followed him through the shop picking up the spare power packs, personal protection shields and the trackers as they went. After picking up all the rest of their purchases and putting them all in the two large rucksacks that they had also just brought, they said thank you to Pete and the cashier and left the shop.

Pete turned to the cashier and said "I hope they are going to be, ok?"

"I'm sure they will, I've remembered where I've seen them. That was Datch and Carina of The Pack, the ones who brought Welly four out of darkness and also saved Arcaneus."

"Bloody hell, and we just sold them guns!"

"Yes, and two weapons tracking systems!"

They both stood starring into space for a moment, lost in their own thoughts before shaking their heads and going back to what they were doing.

Datch and Carina arrived back at the resort and took their new purchases inside the Raven. Datch fetched out the trackers and attached the modules to the rifles and linked them to the Ravens weapons system. He put it in test mode and the ships systems tracked with the guns.

"Well, that works." Datch said triumphantly.

"Cool, so are we going tomorrow?" asked Carina.

"Yes, but let's go after lunch so I'm awake."

"OK, cool."

They got changed into their swim suits and headed to the beach front to get something to eat and spend the afternoon on the beach.

Destination Sol Three

Datch and Carina sat having lunch by the sea under a palm tree. Datch had got his vid com out and was looking at terrain maps of Sol three. It was also showing him the towns and cities. He had found out that the planet had something called the internet that could be used to access all sorts of information. He would still need to be closer to the planet to access it but he figured it would help in finding an ice cream shop. Carina was also looking forward to seeing a primitive species close up. Datch had located a jungle to land in where there were very few villages and very little in the way of civilisation. Hopefully no one would be able to see them come into land and then with the scattering field they should stay invisible to the authorities.

"Well, are we ready to go?" Datch said in an American ascent.

"Sure thing, I'm always ready for an adventure." replied Carina.

They got up and headed to the Raven via the main reception to pay for the stay.

Ten minutes later they were sitting in the Raven's cockpit and Datch was going through the pre-flight checks. Carina was watching him and pressing the odd button or two when Datch asked her to. She was getting quite excited now, this was not only an unexplored planet but also one that had not made contact. She decided to ask her implant what contact was defined as.

'Interstellar contact is defined as either a starship from an unknown planet entering a star system that is already in the IPSF and therefore is contacted as a point of standard protocol or the said race has managed to develop a trans stellar communications system that is compatible with the

IPSF standard systems and therefore is able to communicate directly with the neighbouring star systems. The majority of first contacts are made by ships entering IPSF systems.'

"So, I was just looking up the first contact thing and we don't count do we?"

"No, they have to make the first move. We just ignore them until they do."

"Oh, so we just land, have ice-cream and leave?"

"Well, they do have bars and parties apparently. So, we may have a beer or two as well. Anyway, we're good to go if you're ready?"

"Yes, let's do it."

Datch put his headset on and brought the systems online putting the thrusters in standby.

"Tarasands control, this is the Raven ready for departure."

"Good afternoon, Raven, please state destination."

"We're heading for a bit of sightseeing at Sirius Prime."

"Thanks Raven. Lock on to beacon 724211 and you will be clear to navigate after leaving orbit. Traffic is currently light."

"Thanks, Tarasands, lifting off and locking on to beacon 724211."

Datch brought the thrusters online and the Raven rose into the air. Then he pointed her nose skyward and the Raven headed towards the heavens. Soon the sky outside started to turn a dark blue and then they were in space. Datch followed the beacon to orbit.

"Luyten Control, this is Raven. We are about to drop the beacon."

"Copy that, Raven. Have a safe trip."

"Thanks, Luyten Control, Raven out."

Datch banked the Raven towards the stars and deep space.

"Computer, set course for the Sol star system fourth planet interspace sixteen."

"Please note the star system you have requested is inhabited but has not made contact yet."

"Noted computer. Please continue with commands."

"Course laid in. Journey time will be two hours four minutes. Do you wish alarm thirty minutes before arrive?"

"Make it fifteen minutes please. Engage."

The stars outside winked out and started to flicker.

"Why the fourth planet?" asked Carina.

"I want to do a full tactical scan before going in. I don't want any surprises when we get there. Also, I need to drop an interspace transceiver off. The second one I'll put in orbit above the planet. They should give us a good connection even if it's a little slow."

"Oh cool, so, how long before we can access this internet thing?"

"I didn't think we can do it until we get there."

"Oh, I was hoping to get a heads up on what they are doing now."

"I think we can pull up some of their mass media channels I believe they call it TV. Of course, the closer we get to the planet the more up to date they will be."

"Ok, let's have a look."

Datch pressed a few buttons and an image appeared on the vid panel in the centre of the cockpit. It was a cartoon of a rabbit that seemed to be hitting a duck.

"Err, that's weird." Said Carina.

"Yes, just a bit. let me try again."

Another image appeared and this time it looked like a news reader. They sat and watched it for a couple of minutes. Then Datch tried again this time he found a shopping channel. This was much better; they could see what people were wearing and what styles they had. They also found out the planet was called Earth by the locals and decided the name was more boring than Welly four use to be. This carried on until the alarm sounded stating arrival was imminent.

Datch settled into the controls and then a red dot appeared in the centre of their view and then the Raven dropped out of interspace. There, in front of them was a barren world, red and orange in colour with no life and no oceans. Just dust and rocks. Datch entered a high orbit and brought the scattering field online.

"Computer bring up a tactical plot of the third planet please."

"Compiling please wait."

Datch presses a few more buttons and the news channel came up again. They watched it for about half an hour and then Datch turned to the tactical plot.

"How's it looking?" Asked Carina.

"Well, they are still using their radio waves as detection systems. They also have quite a few satellites in orbit mostly for communication and spying on each other. Also, a couple of orbiting telescopes that could take a picture of us if we were in the wrong place and a very, very, small space station that is about the size of our house. Defence wise, they appeared to be more worried about each other than the multitude of threats from space. At the rate they are going they will get wiped out by an asteroid before they can make contact with anyone."

"Oh, so we can go straight down?"

"Yes, but for some reason there appears to be a couple of crewed interspace signals coming from the northern hemisphere."

"What? I thought they haven't made contact?"

"They haven't, I'm not detecting a ship though, just the signals and they are very weak."

"Could they be the signals your dad went there looking for?"

"Yes, maybe. He never did find anything. They put it down to a small worm hole that was leaking the signals through from elsewhere."

"Well, let's not go to where they are just in case."

"OK, I think if we land in a place they call the Amazon Jungle, we should be well away from anyone. Then we can access this Internet thing and take a few days to work out the best place for ice-cream. How does that sound?"

"I'm good with that."

"Ok, it will be dark there in thirty minutes so let's watch another 'TV' show before we head down."

"That sounds good, Which one though?"

Datch started flicking through the channels and found a show called 'The Grand Tour' that involved three humans trying to drive three machines that kept falling apart.

They watched it and then it was time for planet fall.

Datch turned the Raven and went to interspace factor
three. It took a few minutes to get there and then the planet
appeared. It was a bright blue crescent as they had dropped
out of interspace halfway between day and night. Datch
launched the second interspace transceiver putting it in a
high orbit near a satellite that was transmitting TV to the
humans below. Placing it next to it would make it invisible to
anyone looking up from the planet.

Datch followed the tactical plot and slowly took the Raven
into the atmosphere. The shields caused plasma trails as they
entered the upper atmosphere. Datch reduced the speed to
five thousand KPH and the plasma started to fade. Then they
entered the clouds. Datch descended to two thousand metres
and brought the Raven in over the coast of South America.
City lights could be seen lighting up the city below. Datch did
a few close-up scans to look at after they landed.

The lights became less and less until there was only
darkness punctuated by a campfire or two in the jungle below.
He followed the tactical plot and slowed down. The plot was
only showing animal life for four kilometres. Datch spotted a
clearing up ahead and brought the Raven into land. The
thrusters fired and the Raven dropped down gently between
the trees.

Datch did another area scan for any lifeforms and other
than a few small wild animals and birds there was nothing
about for a two-kilometre radius. He checked the air for
pathogens and viruses. The tests showed that the nanobots
could take care of anything in the air, other than that, it was
good to breathe with similar oxygen contents compared with
Bellatrix. It was lacking some of the argon but that would not
affect their breathing. He activated the external shielding and
shutdown the drive systems.

"Well, we're here and it looks like we have snuck in
undetected." Said Datch.

"Cool. This is exciting." Said Carina.

"Yes, lets head to the rec room and look at images we took on the way over the city and also check out this internet thing."

They got up and headed to the rec room. Datch put the vid of the city up first and zoomed into the streets that they had flown over. He then got them both a drink and sat down next to Carina.

"Computer play the sensor data."

The vid started to show the images from the city.

"Wow, looks like they have plenty of bars and restaurants. Their clothing also looks normal."

"Yes, and it looks like some of them are wearing jackets like ours. So, I think Jeans and T-shirts will be ok."

"We had better get the replicator to make some with English writing on. The Bellatrixian will stand out like a sore thumb."

"Yes. What's that there?" Datch zoomed into a small group of people in a que.

"Hmm, looks like they are getting something out of it."

"That must be the money thing they were using on the TV shows?"

"Yes. We might need to get some of that money stuff. If I connect to my vid com to one of them terminal things, I should be able to get it to give us some."

"Oh cool."

They watched more of the city life. There was a fight being broken up by the local law enforcement that were called 'police'. They spotted a couple of night clubs and a lot of shops. It took about half an hour to go through it all. Then it was time for the internet thing.

"Computer, please connect to the planets internet system."

"Data speeds will be quite slow as this planets communication systems are substandard."

"Ok, noted. Please connect."

"I have selected a search system that the intelligent species has called Google. Please state what you wish to acquire information about."

"Ok computer, please show us information about the area we are currently in." asked Datch.

They watched as information scrolled up the screen. There was a lot of information on it and it took an hour to go through the general bits. Then Datch asked about ice-cream parlours. There was one or two good ones in Brazil but most of the really good ones appeared to be in a place called United States of America. Which was in the northern part of the continent.

"Well, I think we should go camping here for a few days and then go and find the ice-cream." suggested Carina.

"Ok, sounds good. Let's set the camping gear up outside to get the feel of it and have a beer under the stars."

They got up and went to the cargo bay. Datch picked up a large rucksack and opened the cargo bay door. The ramp dropped down onto the ground and they walked down onto the surface of planet Earth. The heat hit them as they reached the bottom of the ramp.

"It's a bit humid, isn't it?" Said Carina.

"Yes, a little. Let's put the camp up over there."

"Ok."

They set the camp up just outside the ship's shields, Datch put up the portable defence shield around the camp and they placed the tent so it was facing their camp fire. Datch put the ships forward lights on so he could find some fire wood and then after lighting the fire turned them off again. They got a couple of beers and sat down on their camping chairs. The stars were out and Datch pointed out Bellatrix to Carina. The jungle creatures were chirping away, creating a nice relaxing sound that reminded Datch of the ones on Bellatrix. They were surrounded by the smells of the jungle that filled the warm humid air.

"This is nice." Carina said relaxing into her chair.

"Yes. We're light years away from any fans and not a member of the galactic press to be found."

Carina laughed.

"So, what are we doing tomorrow?" asked Datch.

"I think we should go that way." Carina said pointing into the jungle.

"Ok, well, I've set the local time into my vid com and its about 10.30pm, so let's get something to eat and then go sleep. I'll set my vid com alarm for just after sunrise."

They went in the ship and came back out a few minutes later with steaks and Kella fries. After the meal they settled down for the night.

"What happens if anyone comes close to the Raven?" asked Carina.

"I have a two-kilometre alert zone set up so if any one comes within it, the ship will send an alarm to my vid com. That should give us enough time to get back to it before it's found."

"Cool."

"OK, Babes, Let's get some sleep. It will be a long day tomorrow."

"Ok."

She cuddled in close to him and after a few minutes they fell asleep.

The next morning Datch's alarm went off and he went to sit up only to find out that Carina's arm was stopping him. After a few moments she stirred and moved her arm allowing him to sit up.

"Is it morning?" she asked yawning.

"Yes, babes. You wake yourself up and I'll go and start breakfast."

"Oh…… O... K..." she said still yawning.

Datch got up and went outside the tent. After placing a pile of wood in the centre of the camp fire he pulled out his plasma pistol. He put in on minimum setting and shot the wood. It burst into flames. He went and fetched some Jeader slices from the ship and started frying them over the camp fire. The smell drifted cross to the tent and moments later Carina came out.

"That smells good." She said walking over to him.

"I thought Jeader rolls would give us a good start."

"They do smell good."

They sat eating the food and having a coffee before packing up the camp.

"So, which way?" Asked Datch.

"Look over there, there's a sort of track."

"Ok, babes, mount up."

They put their rucksacks on their backs and headed off into the jungle. Datch had got a plasma stick which would cut through the jungle undergrowth like butter.

"Is it me or are the rucksacks lighter?"

"The gravity here is only 0.7 that of Bellatrix. So, yes, they do appear to weigh less and also, we are a lot stronger here."

"Oh, cool. This hike should be easy then."

"Yes."

They carried hacking their way through the jungle. A few wild animals came to find out what the noise was but after seeing Datch with the plasma stick decided to go to another part of the jungle and hide under a rock. The animals could sense that there was something strange about them and didn't want to get to close just in case they became dinner.

They came to a thick piece of jungle and Datch put his finger up to his mouth and pointed to the bushes. Carina looked but couldn't see anything. She moved next to him and he pointed though a small hole in the plants. She could just see a brown cat with black spots. Datch got out his rifle and pointed it into the undergrowth turning on the scanner. It showed an image of a large cat on the screen with three kittens feeding. The large cat was staring at them.

'They're so cute.' Came a voice in Datch's head.

'Yes, let's see if we can get an image of them.' Datch thought back.

He got out a little holo cam and sent the little drones round the back of the bushes. The cat crouched down after hearing the noise from the tiny thrusters on the drones.

Datch managed to get the cameras into a good position and took an image of the cats. After he had recalled the cameras, they backed away slowly so as not to disturb them anymore.

"What were they?" Asked Carina.

"I'm not sure, Let's ask the internet via my vid com I've got it connected to the ships systems.

Datch copied the image from the holo camera to his vid com and did a search. A few seconds later the vid com beeped.

"It's called a Jaguar and is a predatory cat that eats other animals."

"They looked so cute though."

"Yes, let's see what else we can find."

Datch put his rifle away and fetched out his handheld scanner and gave it to Carina. She started looking for animal life signs. There was a number of animals ahead of them near a water fall.

Onward they went, moving though the undergrowth. They arrived at the water fall that was cascading down a small cliff to a stream bellow. It was quite wide at the base and the scanner was showing that the water had a snake in it that could be dangerous. They decided not to wade across it but instead Datch found a fallen tree nearby and cut it into lengths using the plasma stick that they could place across the water. Because of the gravity difference the two of them easily lifted the logs into place across the stream.

They crossed it and on the other side they found a small clearing where they decided to have lunch. Up above them there were some brightly coloured birds in the trees and Datch sent the holo cams to get a few images.

Afterwards they sat having a bite to eat.

"So, do you think Tank will find someone this year?" asked Carina taking a bite out of a sandwich.

"I don't know, He was taking to that guy in the Barbers the other week, but I think he's quite happy as he is."

"Fred's dating again."

"Is he?"

"Yes, I spotted him kissing a woman the other day and I've seen her with him a few times now."

"Well, good for him. He needs someone to help him relax. He's been getting quite stressed lately." Said Datch taking a bite.

"I think some of that was the Joining organisation."

"We did give him a few headaches, didn't we."

"So, what did you think of all the gifts?"

"The kitchen assistant was great but we will have to change the kitchen area a bit to fit it in."

"Yes, talking of which, where are we going to put the holo system?"

"I don't know? we may have to add another room on the side of the house."

"Cool. Do you think we can have a splash pool outside?"

"Maybe, I'll talk to my dad about letting us have a bit more land at the side of the house when we get back."

"Cool."

"Anyway, are you ready?"

"Yes, I'm good."

They got up and started heading through the jungle again. They stopped here and there to take holograms of the local wildlife that hadn't run for the hills when it heard them coming.

It got to evening and the light was starting to fade. They had walked about fifteen kilometres through the jungle and had reached a clearing where they could set up camp. Datch cleared a circular area using the plasma stick and after putting the tent up went off to fetch some wood. He arrived back and made a fire while Carina sorted out some food. Datch set up the perimeter shield and as it was now raining set up a deflection shield over the top of the camp to deflect the rain. They sat having a beer and enjoying the evening air even if it was a little damp. The jungle wasn't hot by Bellatrixian standards but it was humid. Datch was recording 29C on his vid com whereas the summer on Bellatrix hit 38C on a normal day and could easily reach 45C on the hotter days. The humidity was very high in this jungle and it made you sweat whereas on Bellatrix the humidity was almost non-existent as the weather service would extract it to make the following mornings rain.

They sat talking about all the things they had seen in the jungle and watched as the rain poured off the side of the shield.

"We don't get rain like this on Bellatrix, do we?"

"I don't know, I'm never up between five and six in the morning when they do the whole rain thing."

"Oh, is that when they do it. I did wonder."

"Yes, we get our rain at that time so it has chance to soak into the ground before the sun gets up. The only exception are the winter storms. They have so much energy, the weather service would have too much trouble controlling them so they just let them run their course."

"I never knew that. Why 5-6am?"

"That was found to be the time when most people are in bed asleep."

"Oh, does it rain in the desert?"

"No, they only make it rain over the land that needs it. The only time the desert gets wet is in the winter storms."

"What about this planet?" she said looking up at the water pouring off the sides of the shield.

"They have no weather control systems and looking at the internet thing they can't even work out where it's going to rain with any certainty."

"Wow. Can we get the TV here?"

"Yes, I've got it on my vid com. I'll get it out. I need to check on the Raven anyway."

Datch fetched out his vid com and pulled up the Raven's tactical view. It showed no humans for a twenty-kilometre radius around the ship but there was a small group about six kilometres ahead of their current position. They appeared to be in some sort of compound. Datch switched to the coms channels and they found a documentary about a city called Los Angeles in the United States of America. They watched the vid for a couple of hours before finally going bed.

The next morning, they got up and had breakfast. Datch pulled up the tactical display on his vid com. The humans were still in the compound up ahead of them.

"Do you think we should take a look at them?" asked Datch.

"Yes, but let's make sure we're not seen, okay?"

"Okay. Put your personal deflection field on just in case they start shooting at things. We don't want to get hit by a stray shot."

"I will, that could hurt a bit."

"Ok, Let's get moving then."

They packed up the camp and started to work their way through the jungle towards the humans. Datch was watching the feed from the Raven's tactical sensors and making sure they didn't get too close to the humans.

They had got within half a kilometre of the human's compound when Datch told Carina to get down. He got out his pistol watching the jungle up ahead of them. His vid com was showing a group of three humans running after another one through the jungle towards them.

Datch and Carina moved to a thick piece of undergrowth looking over a small ravine. Moments later a young woman came running down the ravine with her top torn open and blood on her face. The men stopped and the woman turned to see where they were, a shot rang out. The woman dropped to the ground. The three men came walking down the ravine and went over to the women.

"Is she dead?" Asked one of them.

"No, but she soon will be. Let's leave her for the jaguars." said another.

"Come on, let's head back to the Compound. There are plenty more to have fun with there." Said the third.

They turned and started to head up the ravine back the way they had come. When they were far enough away Datch turned to Carina.

"Come on let's see if we can help," he said.

"Are you sure?"

"Yes, we can't leave her to be eaten by the wildlife."

"Ok, but we had better be careful."

They made their way slowly down to the woman. Datch was watching his vid com all the way but the three men were getting further and further away. They reached the young woman. It looked like her dress had been torn and her top had been ripped open. There was a gunshot wound in her chest.

"Is she alive?" asked Carina.

Datch pulled out his scanner and looked at it.

"Yes, but she won't be for long. The bullets gone though one of her main arteries."

"Can we give here nanobots?"

"Hmm, not sure if they will help but I'll try."

Datch fetched out the nanobots and dropped a pill in her mouth.

"I don't know if they will work as the human's physiology is slightly different to ours."

He sat watching his scanner, very slowly her vital signs started to stabilise.

"Ok, it looks like they are working, the artery is being repaired but it's going to take a long time for her to wake up."

"How long?"

"Hmm. I'm no expert but if I'm reading this right it's going to be at least twenty-four hours I think."

"Well, we can't leave her here then. She'll get eaten."

"Ok, let's take her back to the Raven. The medical unit there can help the nanobots do their job."

"Err… what happens if she wakes up?"

"I don't know. We'll sort that out when we come to it."

They set about making a make shift stretcher out of some branches and a sheet from their bedding. They carefully put the woman on it.

Then slowly they made their way back to the camp site from the night before. When they reached it, Datch looked at the scanner again, her vital signs starting to slowly improve and the artery was being repaired by the nanobots. They set about making the stretcher stronger and strapped the woman in it so that she wouldn't fall out. That way they could step up the pace and get back to the Raven before nightfall.

They hung the stretcher between them and started to walk as fast as they could back through the path that they had made the day before.

This time they didn't have to cut their way through as the path was already there. It took nine hours to get back to the ship. It was nearly dark when they got back. Datch and Carina carried the woman inside and put the woman in one of the spare rooms. Datch set the medical scanner up next to the bed and turned it on.

"How's she doing?" asked Carina.

"Ok, I think. The bots are working but she's lost a lot of blood. If she had been there much longer, she would have died."

"Can we make some with the replicator?"

"Hmm, we would need some fresh blood to copy, but it might work."

Datch looked at the woman's body where the bullet had entered. It was still bleeding slightly. He went off to the ships replicator to get a sterile sample dish. He came back carrying a small tube. The wound was still weeping and Datch placed the tube against it and collected a few drops of blood. He then headed back to the replicator and placed the sample container inside it.

"Computer. Please analyse the contents of the sample container in the replicator."

The sample container vanished and the display showed the molecular structure of the blood.

"Computer. Please make a litre of the substance and place it in a container suitable for injecting into the woman connected to the Medi scanner."

"Please wait."

A small gun shaped item appeared. It was connected via a small plastic pipe to a plastic bag which contained the blood.

Datch picked it up and looked at it.

"Computer. How do I use it?"

"Place the point of the injection gun over the subject's arm and move it about until the indicator turns green. Then press the trigger and hold it until the bag has emptied."

"Thanks computer."

He headed off back to Carina and his patient. When he arrived back Carina was watching her intently but turned around when he entered the room.

"This should help." he said.

He walked over and placed the bag next to the woman's arm and then started to move the gun thing across her skin.

"Are you sure this will be, ok?"

"The computer said it will. So, I'm going with that."

"Ok."

The little light on the gun turned green and Datch pressed the trigger. The blood started to flow from the bag to the gun and disappear into the woman's arm. It took a couple of minutes to get it all in.

"Ok, let's see if we can get the bullet out."

"Are you sure that's a good idea?"

"Well, that's what they were doing on the TV show we watch. That one called ER or something."

"OK, but I thought that was just a show."

"It may have been but it makes sense to remove it."

"Well, if you're sure?"

Datch turned his attention to the scanner.

"This Medi scanner should be able to remove it as long as it's not too big. Its matter transporter is not very powerful but in this case it should do the job."

"Ok, but be careful."

"Right." Said Datch pressing a few buttons.

The little unit displayed in image of the inside of the woman's body in sections. Datch scratched his head.

"Do you know what you're doing?"

"Err, no, do you have any ideas?"

"No."

"Oh, what's that?"

He got the scanner to zoom in.

"Yes, look."

Carina looked at the holo projection and there in the middle of the image was a pointy shaped thing.

"That must be it." said Datch.

"I hope it is and it's not something she needs."

Datch pressed a couple more buttons and then held this hand out under a red arrow that appeared in mid-air. There was a humming noise and the metal pointed object appeared and dropped into his hand.

"There, no problem." He said looking triumphant.

"Yes, no problem!" Said Carina sarcastically.

Datch stood looking at the bullet.

"This is very primitive isn't it." he said.

"Yes, but very effective. Is she ok?"

"Oh, yes, err?" Datch pressed a few buttons, "Yes, the scan says the bots are getting a grip on her physiology now thanks to the scanners input and are repairing her body."

"Good, Can I have a look at the bullet."

Datch passed her the bullet. She looked at it for a moment.

"This could hurt a lot." she said.

"I think it did." Said Datch looking at the woman.

"Oh, yes, sorry." She said turning to look at the woman.

"What are we going to do now?"

"Well, A beer sounds good."

"A beer. What about her?"

"Well, if I tell the Medi scanner to keep her sedated we can get something to eat and drink. Then we can relax and watch the internet thing a bit before going sleep. The system will keep her asleep until we're ready."

"To be honest, I am knackered."

"I am too."

Datch pressed some more buttons on the Medi scanner and it beeped.

"Ok, that's done, she'll stay asleep until we want to wake her."

They turned and headed to the rec room.

"Do you fancy a steak?" Datch asked as Carina sat down.

"Yes, and a starburst please."

"Sure thing, coming right up."

Datch got two plates of steaks and Kella fries along with their drinks. He went over to Carina and sat down.

"Err, I just had a thought. What are we going to do with her?" asked Carina.

"Oh, That's a good point. I don't think we can put her back in the jungle."

"No, not with all the wild animals and human killers about."

"We could take her for ice-cream. I'm sure she would like that."

Carina looked at him for a moment.

"So, the poor woman was attacked and almost killed by a group of humans and then was abducted by aliens, meaning us and taken back to their spaceship where we have performed various medical procedures on her and now you want to take her for ice-cream."

"Err, yes. Everyone likes ice-cream."

Carina looked at him for a moment. Datch meant what he said, everyone did like ice-cream. Carina sighed.

"Ok, but let's talk to her first and if she doesn't have a heart attack, then we'll think about the ice-cream."

They decided to put the TV thing on and try to understand the planet's culture better as it might help in the morning. After a couple of hours, they decided it was quite complex and that they needed to sleep on it.

What are Humans like?

Datch opened his eyes and looked around the room. Carina was in the shower singing to herself. He got up and headed to join her in the shower. Before long they were both feeling refreshed and awake.

"Shall we wake her?" asked Carina.

"Hmm… Let's have a coffee first."

"Ok."

They headed to the rec room and got a coffee from the unit in the corner before sitting down.

"What if she doesn't talk in any of the languages we have downloaded?" Asked Carina.

"Hmm… I don't know?" Datch sat and thought for a minute while taking a sip of his coffee.

"Computer, using data from the Medi scanner connected to the alien. Is it possible to download the Bellatrixian language to the subject's brain without harming her in anyway?"

"The Medi scanner can be configured to carry out the operation and no harm will come to the female being monitored. Please note the operation cannot be reversed."

"So, you mean once we do it, we can't take it back out again?"

"Affirmative."

"We can't do that, can we?"

"Well, what other Bellatrixians is she likely to bump into?"

"Err none, but I'm not sure we should be messing with her head."

"Computer, is it possible to know what language she speaks?"

"Her primary language matrix does not correspond to any known planetary languages."

"Oh… that's a problem then."

"So, we can't talk to her unless we teach her Bellatrixian which would stay in her brain forever."

"Yes."

They both sat looking at the wall for a few moments. Then Datch spoke first.

"Let's teach her Bellatrixian. She's not going to bump into anyone else from our planet, is she?"

"Well, Ok, I know she won't meet anyone else but I'm still not sure we should do it."

"I don't know any other way of communicating with her though?"

"Ok, I don't either."

"Right, let's do it then. Computer, please use the Medi scanner to download the Bellatrixian language matrix to the subject's brain."

"This is not a recommended procedure. Please confirm?"

"Confirmed, please carry out the procedure."

"Procedure underway. It will take approximately ten minutes.

"Time for another coffee then," said Datch getting up.

"What are we going to say to her?" asked Carina after Datch handed her another coffee.

"I don't know. Let's start by trying to put her at ease."

"Yes, she's been through a lot and will still be scared."

"Ok."

They finished their coffees and then headed to the spare room. They went over to the woman's bed and Datch looked at the scanner.

"It looks like almost all of her injuries have healed and according to this, the bot's have fixed a few other bits as well."

"Oh, that's good then."

"The matrix has been installed correctly as well."

Datch pressed a few more buttons and the system did another scan of the woman.

"Computer, please take the subjects measurements and replicate a set of jeans, a t-shirt, socks and some underwear."

"Carina, could you do the honours please. She is a woman."

"You'll have to help a bit though, like holding her up."

"Ok."

Carina went and fetched the items from the replicator and then they set about getting her dressed. Datch held her legs and bum up while Carina put pulled off what was left of her clothes and replaced them with the fresh ones. Datch stood looking at her body.

"Err... Datch I'm here."

"Sorry, I was just interested by the alien body and was wondering if it had all the same bits."

"Well, it does so stop checking."

Datch looked at Carina and then at the woman.

"Ok. Sorry." He said.

He carried on helping and this time made sure he was not looking at anything he shouldn't be. Five minutes later they had finished and the woman was fully dressed.

"Ok. are you ready?" Asked Datch.

"No, but let's do it. Let me take the lead."

Datch pressed a few buttons and the Medi scanner beeped.

The woman started to stir. Slowly her eyes started to flicker open.

"Err…" she said.

"Are you ok?" Asked Carina.

The woman looked at Carina, her mind was full of fear and horror and the memories of the previous morning came flooding back. She went to sit up but Carina stopped her.

"It's ok, just relax. You're safe."

The woman looked at her and a puzzled look crossed her face. She could hear strange noises but for some reason could understand what was being said. She looked at the woman standing next to the bed. She didn't look like a nurse. She put her hand to her chest. There was no bullet hole. But how? She then felt her lip and the cut had gone. Her arm had stopped hurting as well.

"Where am I?" She asked.

"You need to speak Bellatrixian." Said the woman standing next to the bed.

"But I don't speak Bellatrixian." She said in Bellatrixian.

"That's better. My name is Carina and my husband here is called Datch."

"I'm err... Kristina." Said the woman still trying to work out how she was not only able to speak another language but also understanding it.

"OK, Kristina, we were walking through the Jungle when we saw the men chase you and shoot you. We brought you back with us and healed your wounds."

"Oh my, how long have I been here?"

"Err, a little while."

Kristina could tell that Carina wasn't telling her everything.

She looked around the room and spotted Datch standing a bit back from Carina. She started to sit up and then realised she had a very big headache.

"Wow, what happened to my head?" she said raising her hand to her head.

"Err... we had you sedated while your wounds healed. Are you hungry?" Asked Datch stepping forward.

"Yes, very." she said.

She looked at her legs.

"What happened to my clothes?" she asked.

"Err... they were ripped and torn. Also, covered in blood and dirt so we got you some new ones. I hope they are, ok?" asked Carina.

"Yes, thank you."

She couldn't work out what it was but these two people were different somehow. She sat on the edge of the bed. They didn't seem to want to hurt her and they had certainly helped her heal. She must have been out for weeks. Also, her leg felt different where she had broken it when she was younger.

"Here, let me help you." said Carina moving to stand next to her.

Carina put her arm around here and helped her stand up.

"Am I in a hospital? You don't look like doctors."

"We're not as such, but we do know how to heal you."

"Oh, but this is a hospital?"

"Err… not quite, look just come with us and we'll try to explain." Carina helped Kristina to the door with Datch following behind.

The door opened automatically.

"Wow, automatic doors."

"Yes, this is a very high tech err… place." Said Carina.

They went over to the corridor and up the stairs. Datch went first and made sure Kristina could not see into the cockpit.

"In here." he said pointing her to the door.

Kristina went in with Carina and Datch following. The vid was displaying the American TV channel they had been watching the night before.

"Oh, you have cable TV."

"Yes, something like that."

"Would you like a Jeader Roll?"

"Jeader?"

Datch checked his implant.

"Sorry, bacon roll." He corrected.

"Yes please."

"Coffee?"

"Thanks."

Datch went to the unit in the corner and said under his breath "Computer, two Jeader rolls and a cup of coffee please and don't talk about it."

The unit in front of him opened and he took the coffee and Jeader rolls out. He walked back to Kristina and handed her the food.

"Here you are, eat this."

She took a bite. It tasted like bacon but was a bit sweeter than the normal bacon she would have at home. Home, she looked down at her drink.

"What's up? Are you ok?" Asked Carina.

"The men who chased me and." she stopped.

"Yes, we saw them, what happened?"

"Those men, they raped and killed my sister and then tried to rape me. My mum hit the man with a piece of wood and screamed at me to run. I heard them shoot her before they came chasing after me. I ran and ran through the jungle, then there was a shot and a pain in my chest. I fell clutching my chest and everything went black."

"Oh my god. Why would they do that?"

"Because they can." She started to cry.

Carina put her arm around her and tried to comfort her.

"Don't the police stop them?" Asked Datch.

"You're not from around here, are you?"

"Err… no, we are foreigners"

"Well, to answer your question, No. The police are too scared to come this far into the jungle. The drug lord would just kill them." she said sniffling.

"Hmm… this is a crazy planet." Said Datch without thinking.

Carina looked at him.

'Datch, be careful what you say. Remember this world doesn't know we exist.' Came a voice in his head

'Sorry, forgot myself for a minute.'

"Err… well you're safe now. Where are you from?"

"I lived in a small village not far from where you found me."

"You mean live?"

"No. They burnt it to the ground when they took us. They forced the young men and boys to work in the drug plantations and took us for their entertainment. Everyone else was killed."

"Oh, my gods. And no one is able to stop them."

"No. They just do what they want!" She started to cry again.

'I'm going to look at the tactical plot in the cockpit.' Came a voice in Carina's head.

'OK, I'll try and calm her down.'

"I'll be back in a minute Kristina; I need to check on something. If you need anything just ask Carina."

Datch got up and headed to the cockpit. He sat down and pulled up the tactical plot.

"Computer, show any large groups of humans who are armed in the area."

"Please define armed?"

"Carrying fire arms able to kill other humans."

The tactical plot appeared in front of him.

"One group found in local proximity."

"Show me detailed information."

The tactical plot zoomed into an area Seventeen kilometres to the north of their current position which was not far from where they found Kristina. It showed forty armed men in a large compound which had a number of buildings. Also, there were three armoured vehicles and a number of other trucks. A flying machine was parked on a pad at the back of one of the buildings. There were a number of guns set up on the wall that went all around the outside.

"Computer identify the flying machine."

"The aircraft is called a helicopter. It has a top speed of two hundred and fifty KPH and has two rocket launchers mounted on the underside."

"Is it of any risk to the Raven."

"None. The Raven's shields would not be affected by any of the weapons on the tactical view."

"Ok, thanks."

Datch shut down the tactical view and headed back to the rec room. When he arrived, Carina had managed to calm Kristina down and she was just finishing her Jeader roll.

'Well?' Came a voice in his head.

'We're ok babes, they are no threat to us. The computer said that they could throw everything they got at us and they wouldn't even scratch the paintwork.'

'Good, at least we are safe.'

"How are you doing Kristina?" Asked Datch.

"I'm ok, it's just very upsetting. Can I go outside for some fresh air?"

"Err… I think it's raining."

"That's ok, I live in a rain forest remember. It rains all the time."

"Err… there are lots of wild animals outside." Added Carina.

"Again, I live in a jungle. Why don't you want me to go outside?"

"Well, it's not that we don't want you to, it's just that we don't want you upset again."

"Please can I go outside?"

'She's going to find out sooner or later and we can't keep her locked up, can we?' Came a voice in Datch's head.

'Ok babes, but I'm not sure how we're going to explain this.'

"Ok, but please don't be shocked by what you see." Said Carina.

"Will I be?"

"Err… very possibly." Added Datch.

"Ok, follow me." said Carina getting up. "Datch, it may be an idea if you stand behind her in case she faints."

"I'm I likely to?"

"Err… I don't know." said Datch.

Kristina got up and started to follow Carina out of the rec room and down the stairs. They headed along the corridor to the cargo bay.

"This is the strangest building I've ever seen."

"It's not a building." said Datch as they entered the cargo bay. Datch and Carina's bikes sat on one side and there were very strange symbols on the walls that looked like the ancient letters on some of the ruined temples in the jungle.

"Err… what are these symbols on the wall. And what are they?" she said stopping to look at the bikes."

"Let's just go outside, then if you still want to come back in, we'll explain it all. But please don't run off." Said Carina.

"Am I likely to?" Asked Kristina who now knew there was a lot more to these two people than they were telling her.

"I don't know." Said Datch again.

They led her across the bay and Datch opened the cargo bay door. The ramp dropped down and they walked down the ramp. Kristina kept looking up at the underside of the Raven. It was jet black with a number of panels with strange markings on and six large holes with what looked like the ends of jet engines sticking out. They reached the bottom and Kristina turned to look back at the building.

"Oh my god, It's an aircraft."

"Err… not quite." Said Datch.

"Well, it looks like an aircraft."

Then she noticed the engines above her head.

"That's a lot of engines. Are you with the military?"

"No. We're not."

"You seem to know a lot considering you're from the jungle."

"I spent ten years at school in the city. My dad lived there but he died a few years ago and I had to move back to the jungle to be with my mum and sister. Ok I've told you something, now you tell me something."

'Datch, you can do it.' came a voice in his head.

'Thanks!'

"Ok, this is not an aircraft, it is a spacecraft and we are not from your world." Said Datch.

"Really? Do you think I'm stupid?"

'Really.'

"OK, I don't think you're stupid. You're not going to faint, are you?"

"No, why?" She was now starting to think about walking away.

"Ok, you have been here half of one of your days. we have used very advanced technologies to repair your body which was on the edge of death and even your damaged bone in your leg that happened eight years ago. It has healed and is now fully repaired."

Kristina looked at him and then at her leg and then back at the Raven. There was no way they could have known about the broken leg or healed the wounds overnight, also, this craft was very strange and now seeing them in day light they didn't look right either. The woman had purple-coloured eyes and now that she came to think about it, they spoke in a funny way and didn't seem to know much about the jungle. They had asked her a lot of questions but not said much about themselves.

"OK, if you are aliens, where are you from?"

"Well, why don't we go back inside. It is raining."

"This is a drizzle. It's not proper rain."

"Oh, well let's get out of the drizzle then."

"Hmm, you're not going to melt my brain, are you?"

"No, but in case you are wondering, you are now speaking in Bellatrixian. We sort of uploaded the language matrix into your brain so you could understand us."

Datch started to walk back up the ramp.

"You did what!"

"We gave you, our language. You still have your own one and will switch between the two without knowing."

"I will?"

"Yes, come on inside."

"So, what's to stop me running into the jungle and telling the authorities you're here?"

"Well, one you don't even have a scar where you were shot, so the police wouldn't believe that. Two, we are invisible to their detection systems so they can't detect us and we also have a detection system that is keeping a check on all activity in the area. So, if they did come to check we wouldn't be here when they arrived. Therefore, they would just think you were a nut box. I think that's the term used on your planet."

"Oh, I see what you mean. And its nutcase." She said and followed Datch up the ramp.

Carina followed along behind.

'Err, how much do we tell her?' Carina asked in Datch's head.

'Well, we can say what we like, I think? No one will believe her.'

'Ok, but don't make her go mad. Remember she is a primitive lifeform'

'Ok.'

They entered the cargo bay before heading up the stairs and back to the rec room.

"I bet you could do with a drink?"

"Yes, I think I could."

"Do you drink beer?"

"Yes."

"I think we could all do with one." added Carina.

"Computer, two Bellatrixian beers and a Traxsent starburst please."

The unit wined in the corner and the drinks appeared. Datch handed Kristina her drink before passing Carina hers.

"You can tell the computer to do things?"

"Yes, the Raven is fully automated and can pretty much do anything we ask her."

"The Raven?"

"Yes, that's the ships name."

"We have birds called that on this…" She stopped, "err… planet." She added.

"Yes, we have birds called the same on our world. Although, they are a bit bigger." Said Datch.

Kristina though for a moment. And then it hit home. These people were aliens from another world and she was sitting in their spaceship having a drink with them. She felt a little weak.

"Oh my, you are aliens." She said and looked a bit pale.

"Err… have a drink of beer." Said Carina noticing her colour.

She took a very large gulp.

"Better?" asked Datch.

It took a few moments and a few more gulps of beer.

"No, I mean yes, I mean it just hit me, you are aliens."

"Yes." said Carina, "But don't worry we're not here to harm you." she added trying to reassure her.

"So, no sexual experiments?"

"No, why would we want to do that?"

"That's what aliens do, it's on the internet."

"Is it?"

Datch turned to the vid screen.

"Computer, please display internet information about alien contact."

The vid screen lit up and started to show information about alien contact.

"They don't even look like aliens?" said Carina.

"They don't?"

"Datch your dads not been here on one of his nights out, has he?"

"Err, I doubt it, it's two hundred and fifty light years away. Anyway, it's not his style. He does the flashing light in the woods bit."

"Err, what do aliens look like?"

"Well, mostly like us. Some are taller or shorter but the only odd ones are the methane breathers or the arachnoids."

"Arachnoids?"

"Yes, if they came to your planet, you had better work out how to leave and fast. You would be breakfast, lunch and dinner. They like humanoids to eat."

"Haven't you stopped them?" she said thinking the universe was at war.

"They are banned from all the IPSF worlds and if found on one they are exterminated."

"Can't we just shoot them?"

"Err, no. They have built in body armour that can withstand anything other than a direct hit from one of your missile strikes. They are pretty nasty creatures to be honest."

"What's to stop them coming here?"

"Well, nothing."

"Can't you stop them?"

"Well, until you make contact, no."

"But don't worry, they are contained on the other side of the galaxy so they shouldn't get here. The IPSF are very good with keeping them caged in their own star system." added Carina trying reassure Kristina.

"Oh. Ok. So where are you from?"

"We are from a planet called Bellatrix five. We live on a ranch just outside of Yuland city. Computer display images from Yuland city on the planet Bellatrix five." said Datch

The vid screen started to displaying images of home. The city, the city scape, the suburbs, the views looking out over the desert.

"Wow, the sky is green." Said Kristina.

"Yes, we have more argon in the atmosphere than you do. It gives the sky a green tint."

"Oh, wow. That's amazing. Look at the desert."

"We live on the edge of the desert."

"Do you go around visiting alien worlds and testing the aliens or something?"

"Err… no. we don't."

"So, why are you here?"

"We are sort of on our honeymoon and wanted to explore a bit. Mainly somewhere off the beaten track."

"You wanted to explore?"

"Yes."

"So, why did you pick Earth?"

"Err… we wanted ice-cream." Datch looked a little embarrassed.

"Ice-cream?"

"Yes, ice-cream." Said Datch.

"We like ice-cream." Added Carina.

"So, you have travelled millions of light years to get ice-cream?"

"Well, it's only two hundred and fifty light years to Bellatrix and we were actually on a planet twelve light years away sunning ourselves on a beach when we decided to come here." said Datch.

"And you went for a hike through the jungle looking for ice-cream?"

"Oh no, we just wanted to have a look around." Said Carina.

"Oh. so, what happens now?"

Datch sat staring into space for a few moments.

'I know that look.' came a voice in his head.

'Well, we can't just send her back there, can we?'

'Err, you're not thinking of helping her, are you?'

'The Ravens tactical plot said they could shoot at us all day and it wouldn't affect us.'

'Yes, but we would be interfering in the planet's progress.'

'No, it would be just sorting out the bad guys. She said the police were too scared to help them because the drug lord was too powerful. I was just thinking we could cut him down to size a bit.'

'Down to size? You realize they are going to try to shoot us, don't you?'

'Well, we could ask nicely first.'

"Err... what's going on?" asked Kristina

"What?" asked Carina.

"You two are staring at each other and frowning."

"Oh, sorry. We have been given a gift of temporary telepathy and were discussing something."

"You do? Can you talk to me using it?"

"No, sorry, it only works between the two of us and the effect will wear off in a few days."

"Oh. So, what were you two thinking about?"

Datch looked at Carina. Carina looked back.

'Ok. but we have to make sure we clean up any loose ends'

"OK, we're going to help get rid of your drug lord problem." said Carina.

"Good luck with that. You don't happen to have an army, do you? Because you're going to need one."

"No, we don't need an army." Said Datch.

"You don't?"

"No, this ship is armed and has very advanced shielding."

Datch got up.

"Please, just follow me."

Datch left the room and headed to the cockpit and sat down in the pilot's seat. Kristina followed and then stood looking in amazement as Datch called up a tactical view and a hologram appeared in front of them. He then zoomed into the drug lords camp showing all of the humans moving about. The helicopter was missing. Datch did a scan for it and found it heading towards one of the cities.

"It looks like the drug lord has gone to the city for something."

"Oh, well there is no point doing anything until he comes back. We can't cut him down to size if he's not there." Said Carina.

Datch returned the tactical view to the camp.

"Do you know what the buildings are?" Datch asked.

"Some of them."

She started pointing at bits.

"This is where they keep us when we were not being made to work. That is where the drug lord's men live. Also, that's the main house and over there is where they keep all the drugs ready to be shipped to the city."

"Oh, what's that bit?"

"I think they must make the drugs in there. We are never allowed in there and people with white coats would go in and out."

"White coats?" asked Carina.

"Yes, lab coats."

"Lab coats?" asked Datch.

"Err... Overalls?"

"Oh, yes we have them." said Carina.

"Do you have any idea how long it will be before the leader is back?"

"He can be gone for weeks. He only tends to come if there is a problem or a shipment to be taken back."

"Hmm… maybe we need to give him a problem." said Datch.

"We can't just fly over there now. They would see the Raven." said Carina.

"We don't need to; I can target the store and processing plant from here. We just need to take off and get to four hundred metres for the weapons system to get a clear shot."

"You can do that from here?" Asked Kristina.

"Yes, but I think we had better wait until dark so no one see us." added Datch.

"OK, let's head back outside. It looks like its stopped raining, err sorry, drizzling."

Datch shutdown the tactical view and got up. They headed back towards the cargo bay. When they got there Kristina stopped to look at the bikes.

"What are they?"

"Oh, those are our bikes."

"Aren't the wheels a bit small?"

Carina laughed, "No, they fly, the wheels are for landing and take-off only."

"Does everyone have flying bikes where you come from?"

"No, some have cars, pickup trucks, some even have their own ships like the Raven and yes they all fly."

"Wow that's amazing. I'd love to see it someday."

Datch looked at her. She was finding everything amazing. She was looking all over the place fascinated by the ship she was in and didn't seem to be afraid.

"Doesn't this phase you?" asked Carina.

Kristina stopped looking around and thought for a moment before answering.

"A little, but it is so fantastic. I used to dream of space when I lived in the city. I'd sit in the garden at night and look up at the stars but then life caught up with me." She started to look down again.

"Look, maybe we can give you a taste of it after we sort things out here." said Carina trying to cheer her up.

Kristina looked at her.

"You mean you would take me into space?"

"Well, maybe for a little trip."

With that she started smile again.

"But, in return we want to know about your world." Said Datch.

"OK, Deal."

"Deal?"

"Yes, it's a deal."

"Oh, yes. It's a deal."

Datch set up the chairs around a camp fire. It had suddenly burst into flames even though the wood had been wet. He got an extra chair from inside the Raven and they all sat down around the fire.

"So, what do you want to know?" Asked Kristina.

"Well, tell us about the cities, do you know anything about Los Angles?"

"You mean LA, It's in the US. All the movie stars live there. Why?"

"Well, they have a big ice-cream parlour there."

"Oh, they have all sorts of things there. But they are also a little mad."

"Mad?"

"Yes, they do really crazy things."

"Oh. We did see some of the stunts on the tv thing but we thought it was just for the vids."

"Vids?"

"Sorry, TV cameras?"

"Yes, some is, but people do things just to get on TV."

"Why?"

"Well, they just want to be famous I think."

They talked more and more about the planet Earth and they also shared some more information about Bellatrix while being careful not to give too much away. Datch did a barbeque for lunch.

"Wow, these steaks are good." said Kristina tucking into it.

"That's a Jaxx steak from Bellatrix."

"Wow, the meat is so lean. There is no fat on it."

"They are bred for their meat and also milk."

"We have cows for that on earth."

They had the steaks and then pulled up some more TV programs about LA and the North American continent. This time Kristina filled in some of the detail on what was real and what wasn't. It was all really interesting to Datch and Carina. They talked about similarities between things on their two worlds. The afternoon turned into early evening and it started to get dark. The stars came out and they sat looking up into the heaven.

"Which star is yours?" Asked Kristina.

"That one there." Said Datch pointing at Bellatrix.

"Wow, it's so bright."

"Yes, It's bigger than your star. Our planet orbits further out and is also bigger than Earth. Our year is nearly two and a half times as long as yours."

"That's a long year. So does that mean you only live to forty or something?"

"No, each of our bodies lasts for five hundred Bellatrixian years."

"Each of them?"

"Yes, we have five including the one we are born with."

"Wow, so that means you live for err… seven thousand years. Oh my god. How old are you?"

"Err… we are both twelve so about thirty in your years."

"That's incredible."

Datch and Carina looked at each other.

"Err… it's normal." Said Carina.

Datch decided to get away from the chat. He looked up at the night sky.

"Well, I think it's time to ring the drug lords bell." he said.

"Yes." said Carina getting up.

The campfire was extinguished and they picked up their chairs and took them into the Raven.

After giving Kristina a check-up and telling her that the spare room was hers while she was on board they headed up to the cockpit. Carina told Kristina to sit in the seat behind Datch and then sat herself down in the co-pilot's seat. Datch put his headset on and brought the ships systems online.

"How we looking?" Asked Carina.

"All systems are looking good." Said Datch.

Datch put up the tactical view and moved his hand in the holographic view highlighting the production area and the store room.

"Ok, here we go."

Datch brought the thrusters online and then increased power. The Raven started to move, lifting off the ground. Datch checked the scattering field was working ok and that there was no other aircraft in the area.

He pulled back on the power control and the Raven climbed to four hundred metres.

"Computer, bring the weapons systems online and charge the plasma cannons."

The holo screen in front of Datch showed the tactical over lay with the targets highlighted.

"Ok, bell ringing time. Is that right Kristina?"

"Yes, close enough."

Datch squeezed the trigger on his flight control and the Raven shuddered as two plasma bolts were let fly with a flash of green flame.

In the compound one of the men looked up and spotted what looked like green meteors in the sky streaking towards them. A second later the store room and production centre exploded in sheets of green flame throwing pieces of brick work and debris across the compound. The buildings were totally destroyed with only a few bits of wall left standing. The insides were being totally consumed by a green fire and the heat was intense. The men standing next to the buildings became columns of fire as the bodies spontaneously combusted with the heat. Men ran across the courtyard diving for cover as the equipment and chemicals exploded over their heads. Steel frames melted with the heat and one of the armoured vehicles exploded as the plasma fire started to melt it.

Back on the Raven, Datch slowly descended back towards the ground, landing in the same clearing they had just left.

"Was that it?" asked Kristina.

"Computer, what is the status of the targets?" asked Datch.

"All targets have been eliminated."

"Yes." said Datch.

"But it was only one shot."

"Well, two shots at once and they were only at ten percent power."

Datch shut the main drive systems down and put his headset down.

"Well, who fancies a beer?" He asked getting up.

Kristina sat looking at them for a moment. She had expected a volley of shots pounding the buildings not one small flash of light. These aliens had incredible power.

"Kristina, are you ok?"

She shook her head shaking the thoughts from her mind.

"Yes. I just thought it would be more. Err…" She said.

"More what?"

"Well, noisier."

"Oh… No, the weapons don't normally make any noise. That sound was just your atmosphere being superheated as the plasma passed through it. It's a bit like a lightning strike but bigger. Anyway, let's get a beer."

She got up and followed them to the rec room.

Back at the compound men were trying to put out the flames but the heat was so intense they couldn't even get close to the buildings and the water they were spaying at the flames was turning into vapour before it reached them. The green flames burned high into the sky.

A man entered the large house and went over to one of the phones, unfortunately for him it was still working. He dialled a number.

"Hello, what do you want at this time of night?" asked the voice on the other end of the phone in a very annoyed tone.

"Sorry boss, but we have a problem."

"This had better be important. What sort of problem?"

"The store and production facility have just exploded."

"Exploded!!"

"Err, yes."

"Did you find who did it?"

"One of the men said that two meteors came crashing down from the sky and hit the buildings."

"Meteors!!!! I'll be out there first thing tomorrow and I want to know everything. If I find out we have been attacked you will be joining the slaves in the fields. Now find out what happened!"

The line went dead. The man turned and yelled instructions out the door.

Datch and Carina sat talking to Kristina. Carina had just got some food for them and they sat eating hacks wings with fries.

"What sort of things do you do for fun on your world." Asked Kristina.

"We go to a bar for drinks with our friends, watch the sport on the vid and play Solar Ball. Sometimes we'll take the bikes out and fly across the desert or head up to the mountains at Traxsent."

"That sounds really cool, what is Solar Ball?"

"We'll show you after we finish the food if you like?"

"You have it here?"

"Yes, there is a Solar Ball system set up in the cargo bay. We like to use it while going on long trips."

"That's so cool. Is it a video game? I used to have an Xbox in the city."

"Xbox?" asked Datch.

"Video game?" Asked Carina.

"Yes, you play video games on the Xbox."

"Computer please show us the Xbox and define video games." Said Datch.

An image of an Xbox appeared on the vid and the computer started to speak.

"An Xbox is a primitive computer system that is used for playing games. The Xbox sends its output to a two-dimensional display unit called a television."

"Two dimensional? Isn't that a TV?" said Kristina.

"No, not exactly. Computer, please display the jungle outside using the holo emitters."

An image of the jungle appeared on the screen and then expanded outwards half filling the room.

"Oh wow." Kristina said.

She poked one of the bushes near where she was sitting to see if she could touch it. Her finger went right through it.

"That's amazing."

"Are you ready for Solar Ball?" Asked Carina.

"Err, ok." Said Kristina putting the last bit of food in her mouth.

They got up and left the room. Behind them the vid unit turned itself off. They headed down to the cargo bay and Datch went over to the panel in the corner. Moments later the whole bay turned into an alien moon with small creatures bouncing from crater to crater. Kristina stood still looking at the view, awe struck by the sight of an alien world.

"Is it a real place?" she asked.

"It's probably based on a moon somewhere, there are a lot of them but I think the creatures are just made up." Said Carina.

"Ok," said Datch, "Take this and watch what I do."

He gave her what looked like a bat.

Datch stepped up and took an easy shot hitting the white ball into a blue ball which then landed in a net hanging over one of the craters.

"Ok, your turn. Now, I would go for the yellow over there and the net behind it but wait for the creature to bounce off or it could knock it back out of the net." Said Datch.

Carina showed her how to aim. She hit the white ball and it cannoned into the yellow which hit the edge of the net and bounced off.

"Not bad for your first go, just watch the speed, you only have to hit it hard if you want it to go a long way. Watch me," said Carina.

She stepped up and hit the white slowly into a green which went up in the air and gracefully landed in a net.

"You make it look so easy."

"We have had a lot of practice." Said Carina.

"I bet you travel a lot having your own ship?"

"We do get around a bit." Said Datch.

"How many worlds have you visited?"

"Err…" Datch stopped and thought for a minute. The look of concentration on his face was almost painful. He couldn't remember them all. Then he had an idea.

"Computer. How many inhabited worlds have we visited?"

"You have visited two hundred and twenty-seven."

"Wow, that's a lot. Were they like earth?"

"No, some are smaller or bigger. Every star is different and so life evolves differently. But, they were all worlds that were members or becoming members of the IPSF."

"IPSF?"

"Oh, Inter Planetary Space Federation."

"When do you think Earth will join?"

"Err…" Datch looked at Carina.

'A very long time?' Thought Datch.

'Yes, a very, very, long time' Came a voice in his head.

"Well, I don't think it will be for a few hundred years yet, maybe even a thousand." Said Datch.

"This planet is still a bit barbaric by our standards. If men did what those men did on our world the security services would arrest them, scan them and if they were guilty. They would be wiped." Said Carina.

"Don't you mean found guilty?"

"No, their brain is scanned and their memories checked. It shows if they are guilty. There is no doubt when they do the scan." said Datch.

"What, no trial?"

There was a moments pause while Datch asked his implant what a trial was.

"No point, they are either guilty or not."

"Oh, so what is wiped?"

"Wiped. Well, they are taken to a room where their brain is drained of all memories and thoughts before being reprogrammed with a more useful personality that makes them help the society."

"Yes, a few years back a drug baron was wiped and turned into a doctor. After some really bad storms he saved a lot of lives."

"Don't they get their memories back?"

"No, once they are gone. That's it."

"That's some deterrent. I bet you don't get much crime?"

"No, not a lot. Anyway, back to the game."

Datch took his shot making a gentle sweeping movement and knocking a pink into the green putting it in a net. This also left the pink near a pocket.

"Ok, go for the pink. Nice and slow." Said Datch.

Kristina took a slow swing at the white and it sailed majestically into the pink knocking it gently into the net.

"Well done." Said Carina and Datch.

They played the game out making sure Kristina got a few shots in. They had another two games and Kristina was amazed each time a new playfield appeared. After the last game she turned to them.

"I'm guessing when you two normally play, the pace is a bit quicker?"

"Err, yes a bit."

"Could you show me. I'm quite happy to sit and watch."

"OK, if you're sure you don't mind."

"Mind, I want to see it."

Datch went over to the console and pulled up the volcanic moon. Kristina watched as the floor around her turned into molten lava and fissures erupted fountains of lava into a sky that wasn't really there.

Datch went up and hit the white hard, it went shooting into the blue that then smacked into the pink which flew across the bay and into a crater on the opposite side. The unit displayed triple points and then not to be out done Carina hit a triple with the brown, green and blue. The game continued and Kristina watched as Datch and Carina battled it out. The game finished with Carina three points ahead.

"Best of three?" said Datch.

They turned and looked at Kristina who was still transfixed by the game. She nodded.

They continued to play and Datch won the second and the last game came down to the last two balls. Carina was up first and potted the green off the yellow for double points. Datch was left with a triple or a double shot. He went for the triple but missed the third ball instead the ball carried on bounced off a lava bomb and dropped in a crater for a double. The game was a draw making the overall score a draw.

Afterwards they went back to the rec room for a drink.

Kristina started to look tired so Carina took her back to her room and showed her how to manually turn the lights on and off and how to get the shower to work.

After she had got her settled, Carina headed back to
Datch in the rec room. He sat drinking a beer looking at the
TV channels and had found a show called the A-Team.
Carina went over and sat watching it with him for a while.

"Do you think we should be doing this?" she asked.

"I don't think Don would be happy with us, but saying that
we shouldn't really be on Earth."

"Yes, but we're about stop a drug lord because his men
shot a woman."

"Maybe, but just think of all the lives he has destroyed
with the drugs he has sold. We're doing this not just for
Kristina but for all the others."

"Hmm…"

They watched the end of the A-team before heading to
their bedroom. After they had gotten in bed Carina turned to
Datch.

"What are we going to do with Kristina?"

"What do you mean?"

"Well, I think we may have got a bit carried away and told
her too much."

Datch stopped and thought about it.

"Well, we'll ask her to keep our existence to herself and
anyway, who is going to believe her?"

"I'm not sure but she can now speak Bellatrixian."

"Oh… yes… She should stop using it automatically when
we leave though."

"Hmm… I hope so."

"I'm sure it will work out."

He gave her a kiss. They settled down and went off to sleep.

The next morning, Kristina got up and went to the toilet. After having a wee she stood up and turned to flush looking down as she did. She then got very worried, the colour of the waste in the toilet was purple, in fact almost turning towards blue. She flushed and went to sit on the bed checking for anything that hurt. Nothing did. She got up and headed to the rec room to see if she could get anything to eat.

Datch and Carina woke up and after a shower got dressed and headed to the rec room. Kristina was sitting on one of the sofas with a frustrated look on her face.

"Are you ok?" asked Carina walking in.

"The computer won't give me anything." Said Kristina frowning.

"No, you haven't been introduced."

"Oh, can you introduce me?" she said losing the frown.

"Err… no, sorry but you don't have an implant so we can't."

"Implant?"

"Yes, we both have implants in our heads, it's normal on our world. They are a bit like ID cards but built in." said Datch being careful what he said.

"Oh, did it hurt?"

"No, it's totally painless. Just makes your head go fuzzy for a bit."

"So, you can't get the computer to listen to me?" said Kristina with a sigh.

"No, Sorry. It would need to scan your implant."

"Ok, any chance of breakfast?"

"Yes, Jeader, sorry bacon rolls?" Said Carina.

"Yes please."

Carina told the computer to sort out the food and get three cups of coffee as well.

They sat down eating their rolls.

"So, when are we going to stop the drug lord?" asked Kristina eager to get her own back.

"Well, I'm having breakfast first and then I'll check the tactical sensors." Said Datch.

"I take it you're feeling ok today?" asked Carina.

"Yes, but I need to ask you something in private?"

"Ok." said Carina.

Kristina got up to whisper in Carina's ear.

"Err… I went to the toilet this morning and it came out a blue sort of purple colour."

Carina smiled.

"It's fine," she said, "It's just the nanobot's leaving your body and taking the crap with them."

"The what?" said Kristina looking concerned.

Datch overheard their conversion.

"Nanobots, they are microscopic machines that can repair damage to your body. We put them in you when we found you. If we hadn't, you would have died." Said Datch.

"So, these little machines were in my body fixing it."

"Yes, they will repair your body. Any damage they find they fix." Said Carina.

"So, do any stay in me?"

"No. Once their job is done, they exit through the normal process. I mean when you go to the toilet and yes, it looks a funny colour."

"Oh, well that explains my leg then."

"Your leg?" asked Carina.

"Yes, I broke it when I was twelve, but it didn't set correctly and gave me a slight limp. The limps gone and the leg feels like my other one."

"Yes, they will have done that." Said Datch and then added, "Just be glad you hadn't lost an eye, that would have been hard to hide."

"What you mean, I would have got a new one?"

"Yes, they would have made you a new one." said Carina.

"Anyway, I'm going to check on the tactical view. You two finish your food." Said Datch getting up.

Datch got up and headed to the cockpit leaving the two girls alone.

"You know on your world, are there any disabled people?"

"Disabled people?"

"Yes. Look check the internet."

Carina called it up and did a search.

Images of people with missing limbs sitting in wheelchairs, people with guide dog because they were blind and a sign language made for deaf people.

"Oh…" she said looking at the images, "No, any problems are fixed before birth so the child will be born normally and if you are involved in an accident then the nanobots fix it all unless you die."

"Oh, wow, a world without pain."

Carina looked at her for a moment before answering.

"No, not without pain, we have pain, it still hurts when you fall over, it still does when you have an accident and it still hurts when people die." Carina looked into the distance for a moment.

"You have lost someone?"

"I thought I had once and it was horrible, but luckily they survived."

Kristina sensed it was something Carina didn't want to talk about. They finished their breakfast and went to find Datch.

Payback

Datch was sitting in the cockpit looking at the tactical view. There was no sign of the flying machine and the fire had been put out or burnt out, either way it was no longer burning however the remains were giving off a huge amount of heat.

"Computer, do a scan for the flying machine that was in the compound."

It took the computer a few moments before it responded.

"The machine is currently two hundred kilometres away and airborne. It's current heading will see it reach the compound in approximately one planetary hour."

"Show me."

The tactical view chained and zoomed into the aircraft. It was not alone. There were two other aircraft with it.

"Computer. Identify the other two flying machines."

"The other two aircraft are also helicopters. They are also armed. Both are equipped with primitive rocket launchers and one has three machine guns."

"Are they any threat to us?"

"No. They will not be able to penetrate the shields."

"Show me the compound again."

The tactical view switch back to the compound.

Datch sat looking at it, studying the layout.

Just then Carina came walking into the cockpit.

"How's it looking?" She asked.

"Ok, the drug lord is on his way and is about two hundred kilometres out, oh, and he's bringing friends to the party."

"What do you mean?"

"Computer. Show the aircraft and give me visual."

The Tactical view switch back to the three aircraft and the vid in front of Datch came on displaying the aircraft flying in formation.

"How can you do that? Wait, that's a gun ship." said Kristina suddenly looking worried.

"Oh, is it. I thought it was a helicopter." Said Datch.

"It is, but it's also very heavily armed."

"No, it's not." Said Datch.

"Wait, it's not?"

"Well, it might be by your standards but not by ours." Said Datch.

"It only has very primitive weapons. Without shields it could be deadly but we have them." said Carina.

Datch pressed a few buttons and the weapons systems came online.

"Computer, please enter these targets into the weapons system for execution later."

He selected the aircraft and then switched the tactical view to the compound. He then selected the remaining gun emplacements that had survived the fires, the main gates, a truck with a machine gun on the back and the main house.

"There. That should do it."

"You're going to destroy it now?"

"No, I'm going to ask him to leave first."

"You're mad. He'll shoot you."

"You mean he'll try. Anyway, if he does the rest will be self-defence."

"Self-defence? Really?" Asked Kristina.

"Yes." said Datch.

He got up.

"Right, it's going to be an hour before they get here so let's say we go in about two hour's time. It will give him time to upset his men. Let's go and look on the internet for more ice-cream parlours."

"You do know you need money to buy ice-cream, don't you?" said Kristina.

"Yes, we need to find a town or city in the USA with a cash machine?"

"A cash machine? You need to have a bank account with a cash card to use one of them."

"I don't." said Datch grinning.

They headed off to the rec room in search of ice cream parlours.

An hour later the drug lords helicopter arrived at the compound and hovered for a while looking at the damage to the buildings that had been hit. The pilot had to keep the helicopter away from the remains of the buildings as the heat was affecting the aircrafts stability. The drug lord looked down. There was nothing left, even the metal work had melted and formed pools of what looked like liquid metal in what was left of the structure. There was very little left of the walls as well. Just the odd pile of half melted bricks.

The drug lord signalled all the helicopters to land. They dropped down inside the compound and landed. The drug lord stepped out and was greeted by a wave of heat coming from the remains. A man came running over.

"Welcome boss, please follow me." he was looking very jumpy and nervous.

The drug lord followed the man over to a group standing near the house.

"Hello boss, sorry about this."

"This is a big setback. I need this place up and running in a week. I have told my customers we had a fire and it destroyed part of the labs but we should be back up and running in a couple of weeks."

"Boss, we can't even get near the building yet. The heat is too intense. We shoved one of the slaves into one of the buildings and he burst into flames instantly."

"It can't be that hot."

"It is, watch."

He shouted at the men. Another slave was brought out and taken towards the building. The men then pointed at the building but the man wouldn't go. They shot him in the arm and the man shouted. Then two men grabbed him and flung him towards the building. He couldn't stop himself in time and fell through what was left of a wall. He screamed as he burst into flames and collapsed. Moments later there was nothing left but ashes.

"Have you tried putting water on it?"

"Yes. Watch."

He nodded to two men holding a large hose pipe. They turned it on full and a powerful jet of water went towards the remains. As the water crossed the building's threshold it instantly turned to stream and shot up in the air.

"And there were no attackers?" he asked.

"No. It was a quiet evening and I sat playing cards with a couple of men. Then two balls of fire came crashing down from the sky. No noises other than the normal jungle animals. The balls of fire hit the buildings and they burst into flames."

The drug lord looked at the remains and could see the heat being given off and rising into the air. He thought to himself. No weapons that he knew of could do that. Even if high explosives started the fire, they would have been able to put it out with water. He looked up at the sky. This was not his day. His buyers were violent men and had threatened him. They were ready to switch suppliers if he didn't find the goods and that would not go well for him.

"Ok, we'll have to use the slave's quarters for the labs and the slaves can sleep in a camp outside the compound. Get them to start building one. I'll go and sort out some more lab equipment. Go get the slaves moving. Now move it!"

"Yes sir!" Said the man looking relieved.

The drug lord headed into the house to make some calls.

Datch looked at the time, an hour and a half had gone by.

"Well, looks like it's time to pay our friends a visit." he said.

"Is it that time already?" Asked Carina.

"Yes, let's go and ask them nicely to leave." Said Datch with a grin on his face.

Kristina looked at them both, they were both enjoying this. It seemed to be exciting to them.

"You do know that they won't go, don't you?"

"They will be going." said Datch still grinning.

They headed to the cockpit and Kristina sat down behind Datch. Carina sat herself down in the co-pilot's seat.

Datch brought all the systems online and went through his check list. He then brought the weapons online and checked to make sure the targets were still selected. Finally, he powered up the shields and extended them so that they radiated out from the ship by five metres.

"Ok, is everyone ready?" He said.

"Well, not ready but let's go." Said Carina.

"Are you sure we'll be safe?" Asked Kristina.

"Yes, we are totally safe." Said Datch.

He checked the tactical view for any other aircraft or vehicles in the area. There wasn't anything that could see them so he increased power to the thrusters and the Raven lifted off.

"How are we doing this?" Asked Carina.

"Well, we're going to park outside his front gate. Leave the Raven and ask them to leave." Said Datch.

"They will start shooting at us." Said Kristina.

"They might try." Said Datch.

Datch turned the Raven and headed to the compound.

The drug lord was in the main house when he heard shouting outside. He got up and went out just in time to see a large black aircraft fly over the top of the compound. It was black with green flames down the wings. He looked at it. It wasn't like any other aircraft he had seen. It slowed and turned facing towards the main gates. The drug lord headed to the gates with his men. They were all armed. He nodded to the helicopter pilots and they started their engines.

Datch brought the Raven in for a soft landing about fifty metres from the gates. He then got up and picked up his rifle.

"You're not going out there?"

"Yes. It should be fun like the A-team." He said grinning.

"Yes." said Carina getting up.

Kristina reluctantly followed them down to the cargo bay.

Datch opened the door and they walked down the ramp. He turned at the bottom and headed to the front on the ship. The drug lord walked out of the gates with his men.

"Ah, you must be the main man!" Said Datch raising his rifle.

The drug lord stopped and his men raised their guns.

"Who the fuck are you?" he said.

"We are the people who are going to get you to leave this jungle and never come back. Also, please don't swear there are ladies present." said Datch.

"I don't care what the fuck you think. Did you destroy our buildings?"

"Yes, and we will destroy you if you don't leave."

"What the three of you." He laughed.

"Yes." Datch stared at him and that made him worry for no apparent reason.

"Well, why don't we shoot you and take your fancy aircraft." he said laughing and turning to his men.

"Try it!" Said Datch.

The drug lord lifted his gun and shot it at Datch. The bullet hit to shield and ricocheted off it hitting the wall near the gate.

"Hmm, missed." Said Datch and grinned.

"Kill them!" Shouted the drug lord.

Gun fire erupted as all the men with the drug lord opened fire. Kristina closed her eyes and waited. There was a lot of screams and shouts. The bullets hit the shield and were deflected backwards hitting men, walls and pretty much anything in the opposite direction to where the bullets were meant to be going. One hit the drug lord in the arm. Most of his men were killed by their own bullets and the rest were injured. The drug lord backed towards the gate.

"Destroy them and the aircraft." he yelled.

"That's a pity. I was hoping they would go." Said Carina.

Kristina opened her eyes and looked at the carnage in front of the gates. Bodies of the men were laying where they fell and the injured ones were trying to get back into the compound.

The two remaining gun emplacements now opened fire at them and made a lot of holes in the walls and gates. The three helicopters took to the sky above the compound and fired their missiles at the Raven. They hit the shields and exploded taking part of the compounds wall out in the process. Datch turned to Carina.

"Do you think they are trying to harm us?" He asked.

"I think so." said Carina.

Kristina stood there in disbelief as the drug lord threw everything he had at them.

"So, if we open fire, it will be self-defence?" he said as another round of missiles hit the shields.

"I would say so." Said Carina.

"Are you two for real?" Asked Kristina.

"Yes!" Said Datch. He lifted his rifle and pressed the trigger.

Above their heads the forward pulse cannons dropped down from inside their pods and opened fire. Two bolts of green plasma vaporised the gun emplacements and most of the wall under them sending bits of wall flying into the air. Then two more bolts of plasma hit the gunship and one of the other helicopters. They exploded into a million pieces, nothing but tiny pieces of metal fell to the ground. The third helicopter tried to turn in an attempt to escape but the cannons fired again sending it and the front gates to oblivion.

The next volley took out the trucks in the compound vaporising the wall in the process. The drug lord started to run for the house. Then the cannons fired again and the house exploded in green flames reaching high into the sky. The drug lord hit the deck as bits of building few over his head. A large piece of brick work landed on his legs smashing them. He screamed as the brick work rolled across them.

His remaining men leaped into the last of the pickup trucks and tried to make a run for it. The drug lord screamed at them to come back but they drove towards the hole that had been the gates trying to escape. Datch pointed his rifle at them and pressed the trigger the cannons fired again vaporing the truck and the remaining section of wall.

Datch looked around.

"Computer, how many targets are left?" he said into a comms unit.

"One human target remains. Do you wish it eliminated?"

"No. I'll take care of it."

Datch turned on his personal protection shield on and set the forcefield to maximum.

"You can't go out there." Said Kristina. "He'll shoot you."

"I have a personal shield. Any bullets will bounce off."

"Here, put this on." Said Carina passing Kristina a small backpack.

She put it on and Carina showed her how to activate it.

"Err, it smells funny." she said.

"Yes, it's set up for our atmosphere, don't worry its ok for you to breath. You'll get use too it soon." Said Datch.

Carina raised her gun and they walked forwards towards what was left of the compound. As they stepped forward through the shield it fizzed around them as they passed through it.

There were bodies and burning wreckage littered about in what remained of the compound. They walked past the craters where the trucks had been and over towards the blazing inferno that was a house. The drug lord was trying to crawl away from them dragging his legs behind him.

"And where do you think you're going?" Asked Datch as they reached him.

He turned to face them and pointed his gun at them.

Datch smiled at him.

"You really think that will work?"

The drug lord looked at him and threw the gun away.

"Who are you?" he asked still trying to back up.

"We are your gods." Said Datch.

"You have defiled the sacred jungle." said Carina joining in.

"Your men left this woman to die in the jungle after killing and raping her sister and killing her mother."

"My men take care of things for me. I don't tell them what to do."

"Well, you can't now. They are all dead." Said Carina.

"All." said the drug lord looking around.

"All!" Exclaimed Datch.

"What are you going to do with me?"

"We are going to leave you to the men you used as slaves."

"They will kill me!"

"Yes, very likely. You had better hope they make it a quick end." Said Carina.

"You have no doubt killed many people. What is that saying on the internet. People who live by the sword, die by the sword." Added Datch.

Just then some of the men who had been slaves came around the corner. They looked at the three of them standing over the drug lord and then spotted Kristina. They came over a little apprehensively.

"Kristina?" said one of the men in her native tong.

"Yes, this is the man that enslaved and killed us." she said.

"Tell them they came have him." said Datch.

"Do what you want with him." Said Kristina.

Two men grabbed his arms and dragged him out to the jungle screaming.

All they heard were the screams and then after a few minutes it went quiet.

"Kristina, are you coming?" Asked one of the men.

"No. I don't want to be in the jungle anymore, my family are dead and the jungle will always remind me of that. I think I need to be in a city." She looked at Datch and Carina.

"Well, I suppose you can come with us for ice-cream." said Carina.

"OK." said Datch.

"I think this place could make a nice village if you cleaned it up." said Carina.

"Tell them to wait a week for the plasma fires to cool down though." Said Datch.

Kristina relayed what Datch had said to them.

"Do you know anywhere with nice views. We sort of want to take some pictures of the jungle to show them when we get home?" asked Carina.

"Don't you need to move the Raven?" Asked Kristina.

"Not until dark. We can block your radar but it won't stop people seeing it and taking picture of it."

"Oh, I see what you mean." said Kristina.

"So, how are we going to get to a city?"

"I have a plan." Said Datch grinning.

"Ok." Said Carina.

"Ok?" asked Kristina looking at Carina.

"Yes, when Datch has a plan, it will normally work." said Carina.

"Right, let's go find some nice views." said Datch making sure they changed the subject away from later.

Kristina led the way off into the jungle via the Raven as they needed the bathroom and to get their vid coms and jungle stuff.

They spent the next ten hours taking pictures of animals and birds. The jungle was a bit easier to walk though as Kristina knew where the paths were. Also, Kristina took them to a high vantage point for some stunning vistas across the forest and Amazon River as it meandered its way through the jungle. They were able to see red howler monkeys, giant river otters, black-capped squirrel monkeys, a sloth hanging from a tree that appeared to be asleep and a collared anteater who was currently make a meal out of an ant hill.

Finally, they got back to the Raven. The remaining men and women from the village were currently making the compound their home. The bodies in the compound had all been thrown into the plasma fires to get rid of them. They had cleared out all the stuff that the drug lord's men had and had thrown it in with the bodies. The plasma fires were still burning with large intense green flames and consumed everything. That is apart from some of their clothes that various members of the tribe where now wearing. They had also acquired a large number of guns which were now piled up outside of the storeroom. The storeroom that had become quarters for the men was now being converted into homes for the tribe. A second fire had been lit in the centre of the compound which now had a wild boar roasting over it on a makeshift spit.

One of the men came walking over to them and said something in their language.

"What did he say?"

"He wants us to stay and have some food with them."

"Oh, OK, tell him we would be very honoured but it will have to be a light snack as we need to leave when it gets dark."

Kristina explained to the man who then turned and shouted to the others. The compound became a hive of activity and seating of one sort or another was laid out in a semi-circle around the fire. The tribe gathered together and then the head of the tribe stood up in front of the fire and started to speak. Kristina translated for them.

"He says. The tribe will be forever in your debt and that they are very grateful to you for saving them. If you ever need a home then you will always be welcome by the side of their fire."

"Tell, him thank you and they are all wonderful people and it was an honour to help them."

She did and the man walked over to one of the other men who was holding a bow with a small bag containing arrows. He took them and walked back to Datch. He said something and held out the bow and arrows.

"He says, Please accept this bow. It is the tool of a great warrior. May your arrows be true and may the gods light your path."

Datch bowed towards the man and took the bow and arrows.

"Tell him, I wish their tribe to grow and prosper and may they all live long and happy lives."

The leader smiled and clapped his hands and some metal plates came out from somewhere. They were all handed one and Datch was given a knife. The man gestured to the boar.

"He wants you to take the meat first. You will have to get ours as well as the woman is owned by the man once the man has taken the woman."

Datch took Carina's plate and Kristina's. Then walked across and cut off a number of pieces of meat placing them on the plates. He then bowed and took the food back to the girls. Afterwards each of the men went up and took meat from the boar.

They sat on some deckchairs that had survived the destruction and started eating the meat.

"This is quite good meat, reminds me of barbequed Jaxx. I just need a Bellatrixian ale to go with it."

"I could go and get some." Said Carina.

"No, it's OK. I need to keep a clear head for the flight."

The leader looked at them.

"Tell him the meat is very good and it reminds me of home."

Kristina did and the leader smiled.

They finished the meat and sat talking to the tribe. It started getting dark and Datch stood up and walked over to the leader with Kristina in tow. The man looked at him.

"We must be leaving now. Thank you for the food. I will remember you and your tribe forever."

Datch held out his hand as Kristina translated

The man looked at his hand and put his hand in Datch's.

"And you will be in ours." Kristina translated.

They shook hands.

The man turned to Kristina and said something and there was a brief conversation before the man nodded to her.

"What did he say?"

"He asked if I was sure I didn't want to stay. I told him I was going with you."

Carina stood up and went over to Datch and Kristina. The tribe also stood up.

"Kristina, tell them that we have to go now and to take care of themselves."

They said their goodbyes and the tribe watched as the left the compound.

They headed inside the Raven, Datch closed the cargo bay door and the ramp lifted up. They headed to the cockpit.

What Aliens?

Datch sat down in the pilot's seat and brought the systems online. Kristina sat down behind him and Carina headed for the co-pilot's seat.

"Err, so what's the plan?" Asked Carina sitting down.

"Well, I've been doing a little research."

"And?"

"Well, all alien craft on the internet are bright glowing discs in the night sky. Therefore, it's only the posers who are seen."

"And how does that help us?"

"We're in a black ship that unless they see our rear end, they won't spot us."

"We're going to a city though?"

"Yes, it's dark and I have a plan."

"Ok?"

"But we need to make a stop first for money."

"And where are we going to do that?"

"Roswell in the United States." He said with a grin.

"Why there?"

"It's a city that celebrates a UFO crash and lots of people go around dressed as aliens. So, we'll fit right in."

"Won't they notice a great big spaceship parking in the centre of their city?"

"Yes, but we're parking out of town and taking the bikes in."

"We don't have flying bikes yet." Said Kristina feeling she should add something to the conversation.

"I know, that's why we're going to pretend to use the wheels through the city where we can be seen." Said Datch.

"Our bikes look nothing like the ones on this planet."

"They do there. Computer display images of Roswell carnival on the co-pilot's vid."

Images of the Roswell carnival appeared on the screen. They showed bikes, cars and even people dressed up to look like flying saucers. They had coloured lights on them and looked like they had been created by someone who had been drunk at the time of the design stage.

"Oh, I see what you mean." Said Carina.

Kristina had to agree the bikes would fit in.

"OK then, it looks like about six thousand kilometres away. I'll take us up high away from other aircraft. Computer, scattering field status?"

"Field is operating normally."

"Ok, then here we go."

Datch increased power to the thrusters and the Raven lifted off. He pointed her nose up and increased power to the main engines. The Raven shot into the sky climbing higher and higher.

Kristina watched as the ships display read out all sorts of data that meant nothing to her and then out of the windows as the stars got brighter.

After a few minutes she asked, "How long will it take us?"

"Hmm... about thirty minutes," replied Datch.

"I thought you said it was six thousand kilometres away."

"I did."

"Wow. how fast are we going then?" She asked,

"Err, we are currently at just over eleven thousand kilometres per hour and we will reach a cruising speed of fifteen thousand kilometre per hour in about thirty seconds. We are also at an altitude of seventy thousand metres."

"Are we in space?" she asked looking over Datch's shoulder and seeing a bright semi-circle to the left showing the curve of the earth.

"No, not quite, that's another fifty kilometres higher but we are well above the normal air traffic and most of the atmosphere."

Kristina was transfixed by the view outside. The blue crescent with the sun shining across the edge and lighting up the cloud top. The sight was magical to her. She watched as the last rays of sunlight hit the cloud tops sending beams of orange light across the evening sky. She looked out the opposite window and could see stars shining bright in the night sky. She turned back to the sun side watching the sun as it started to sink behind the planet.

It was at this point the Raven flew straight over a SETI installation. One of the scientists was looking at the data coming in from the huge radio telescope outside. The random data kept scrolling up the screen and he totally failed to notice that a couple of digits had repeated eight times in a row. Which was a shame as he had spent the last ten years of his life working there looking for it. He got up and went to make a cup of tea checking on the way to see if there were any interesting snacks in the vending machine. He went for a bar of chocolate.

The Raven thundered through the thin upper atmosphere. Down below the humans were totally oblivious to its existence including the ones looking up. NASA was talking to the International Space Station and got a bit of a squeak on the audio. NORAD totally failed to see them and an amateur astronomer thought for a moment he had found a new black hole.

Datch started to descend dropping the Raven down through the atmosphere. Kristina watched as the sun vanished behind the planet plunging them into night. Outside the shield started to light up with plasma.

"Err, don't you think they might see us?" asked Carina.

"Ah, good point."

He slowed the Raven a bit more and the plasma started to fade.

Down below several people wished on a shooting star that wasn't.

"There that should do it, we're down to five thousand KPH."

The plasma disappeared.

The Raven dropped down towards the normal flight lines. Datch was watching in his heads-up display for aircraft making sure he gave them a lot of distance. They were now over the USA and the flight lanes were very busy. There weren't any landing beacons here and plenty of things to hit. He slowed the Raven again to three hundred KPH and levelled out at six hundred metres.

"Computer, please identify an area just outside the city on the tactical view where we can land without being seen."

The computer started a detailed scan and after a few moments highlighted three areas on the plot.

"These are all uninhabited areas."

Datch looked at them and selected one inside some trees and a long way from any humans. He changed course and headed to the west of the city. The lights of the city could be seen to the right as they approached the landing site. Datch was using the sensors to see and brought the Raven in for a landing in amongst a group of trees that were growing in a small ravine. He shut the systems down and had a look at the tactical scan for signs of movement.

"OK, it looks good. Let's go get some of this money stuff." Said Datch getting up.

"Err, I don't speak American by the way." said Kristina.

"What language do you speak then?" asked Carina.

"It's called Portuguese."

"Oh, ok, if anyone asks, you're a friend from err, South Brizil?"

"No, not south. It's part South America. It's just Brazil. Br a z il."

"Ok, Brazill?"

"Good enough."

They reached the cargo bay and Datch got on his bike.

"Carina, if you take Kristina on your bike, I'll fly us to the edge of the city using my sensors. No lights, ok?"

"Yes, ok. What are we doing when we get there?" Asked Carrina.

"Well, I'll scan for one of the money machine things. Then we put the lights on and head to it. We'll fly just above the ground so it looks like we are riding along the road."

"And you're sure the noise from the bikes won't give us away?" asked Carina.

"Some of the bikes in the city in Brazil made that much noise you couldn't hear the planes in the sky. Oh, and the cash machines are called ATMs." Added Kristina wanting to help.

She climbed on behind Carina and they started up the bikes.

"OK. let's go." Said Carina.

Datch pressed a button, the cargo bay door opened and they headed outside. Once outside Datch instructed the ships computer to keep the shields up and to notify him if any humans started to approach the ship.

"Ok, Carina you ready?"

"Yes, I've set my bike to follow yours."

Datch increased power and the bikes took to the air. Kristina looked down.

"Oh my!" She said, "we're flying."

"Yes, why?"

"Err, just I 've never flown before."

"You have just flown six thousand kilometres."

"Yes, but that was inside an aircraft. What happens if I fall off?"

"Try it." said Carina.

"You want me to fall off?"

"No, we want you to try to fall off. You won't be able to."

Kristina gingerly tried to lean over a bit too far only to find out there was an invisible wall stopping her. She tried a little harder. Still the same effect.

"Wow, there is something stopping me." She said.

"Yes, the bikes have forcefields around them to make sure we're safe. Even if there is an accident, they will protect us." Said Carina.

"The bikes also have avoidance systems, so other than a speeding UFO, nothing will hit us." Added Datch.

"We are the speeding UFO's!" Said Kristina.

Datch gave the bikes a kick of speed and the bikes thundered across the fields.

A farmer came out of his house to see what the noise was but by the time he had come out the door the bikes were already in the distance. He turned and shouted at the door,

"Margret, the bloody air force is doing night missions again!"

He turned and watched the tiny lights disappear before heading back inside muttering to himself.

The edge of the city could be seen up ahead. Datch slowed right down and came to a stop just inside a farm track leading onto one of the main roads. He fetched out his hand scanner and started looking for the ATM. He found one about two kilometres inside the city that appeared to be fairly free of people.

"Ok, I've found one. I'm setting the bikes to one centimetre off the ground. Remember if anyone asks us, the bikes are being dressed up for the next carnival. Ok?" he said.

"Ok." said Kristina.

'You sure about this?' Came a voice in his head.

'Yes, no problem' He thought back to Carina.

He set the bikes to fifty kilometres per hour and they headed off into the city.

The streets were quiet in the suburbs with only a few people milling about. One or two people looked at the bikes as they went by but other than an odd wave, no one was bothered. Datch followed the navigation system that was mapping the city as they went. They came to an area with a couple of bars, a number of shops and more to the point a bank with a ATM. Datch slowed down and pulled up outside the bank. Carina parked next to him.

'Should we be doing this?' Came a voice in Datch's head.

'Yes, it will be fine. It's a bank, they won't miss a little bit of this money stuff. I'm sure they have plenty of it.'

Datch got off his bike and turned to the girls.

"I'll be right back." he said.

He walked over to the ATM and got out his vid com placing it on the ATM's keyboard. It took it a few moments to sync with the ATM's computer. He selected the vending diagnostics and then told the ATM to start the vending system. Paper money started to come out the machine and Datch put it into a bag he had brought with him. He let it vend for two or three minutes until he spotted a human male heading towards the bank. He stopped the ATM vending and put it back into normal operation. He gave the person a quick look to check if he had seen anything before going back to sit on his bike.

'Did you get it ok?' Came a voice in his head.

'Yes, I got just under twenty thousand dollars I hope it will be enough.'

"Ok, all sorted. I'll put some in the bike. Do you fancy a beer?"

"Well, I wouldn't mind one, but will the bikes be, ok?" asked Carina.

Just at that point the man at the ATM turned and started to walk over.

"Cool bikes dude."

Datch looked at him. He didn't seem to be hostile.

"Thanks, dude. We're getting them ready for the next carnival."

"They look great. I love the shape. They look like they could really fly. Though if you don't mind me saying dude, they may need a few more lights to win the top prize."

"We were planning to put a few more on." Said Carina.

"Yes, make them nice and bright. The judges love lights dude." Said the man.

"Err, dude we're from just outside the city. We're looking for a quiet bar to have a drink and maybe something to eat, do you know any?"

"Sure, that one over there can get a bit noisy but if you go to the one just down there. It's a nice chilled atmosphere and they do food." He said pointing down the street a bit.

"Ok, sounds good, thanks dude."

"No problem, dude and I hope you do well at the carnival."

"Thanks dude."

Datch started his bike and Carina followed suit. They turned and headed off down the street. The man watched them go and then went off looking for another ATM as that one seemed to have developed a fault.

Datch spotted the bar and pulled into the parking lot next to it.

"How much do you think I should take in?" asked Datch.

"Err, say fifty to a hundred dollars." Said Kristina.

"Is that all?"

"Yes, why? How much did you get?"

"Err about twenty thousand."

"How much!"

"Twenty thousand." Repeated Datch.

"Why is that a lot?" asked Carina.

"Err, yes." Said Kristina.

"Oh, does two hundred sound, ok? That way we should have plenty."

"Yes, what are you doing with the rest?"

"I'm putting it in the front compartment."

"Someone might steal it." Said Kristina.

"Technically, someone just did." Said Carina.

"No, it will be fine, the bikes have similar forcefields to the ship. No chance of them getting past it."

"Oh. Will it hurt them?"

"Only if they try to hit it."

Datch got off his bike and sorted out the money, shoving a number of bills into his pocket. Carina and Kristina got off their bike and after Carina had set the anti-theft systems, they walked over to Datch who was doing the same.

"Ok, so, do we go straight to a table or wait for someone?" asked Datch.

"I'm not sure, different places have different ways of doing things." said Kristina.

Just then a car pulled into the parking lot and a man and a woman got out.

"Let's follow them and see what they do." said Carina.

"Good idea." Said Kristina.

The man and woman walked in and stood near the door waiting. There was a sign saying 'Please wait here to be seated'. The three of them went in after and stood behind them. A few moments later a tall woman with a pink and white pinny on came over to them.

"Hello, Can I help you?" she asked.

"Yes, we would like a table for two please?" Said the man

"Certainly, please follow me."

She led them over to a table on the opposite side of the bar and got them seated before coming back to Datch, Carina and Kristina.

"Hello, Can I help you?" she asked.

"Yes, we're after a couple of beers and some food." said Datch.

"Certainly, please come this way."

She led them over to a four-seater table next to a window and they sat down.

"I'll be back in a few moments to get your order. These are the menus and the drinks are listed on the back."

"Ok, thanks." Said Datch.

She went back over to the other couple.

Datch picked up the menu and looked at it.

"Wow, it's all written on parchment." He said quietly.

"It's not parchment, it's paper." Said Kristina.

"Oh…"

He passed a menu over to Carina and then went to pass another to Kristina.

"Err, It's in English. I can't read it." she said.

"Sorry."

"I'll read it to you." said Carina.

She went through the menu whispering in Kristina's ear.

"Well, I'm going for the steak." Said Datch.

"Yes, me to." Said Carina.

"Ok, me as well." said Kristina who wasn't sure what the rest was.

"What about drinks?" said Carina.

"Kristina, do you know any?"

She looked at the back of the menu.

"There is Budweiser. They have that in Brazil and it's like the Bellatrixian ale we were drinking. I don't know the rest."

"Ok, we'll go for that."

The waitress came back and asked them for their food and drinks order. Datch decided large beers were in order.

A few moments later the waitress came back with three large beers.

"Here are your beers, the food will be about fifteen minutes."

"Thank you," they all said.

Datch looked at the beer in front of him. It was in a tall glass with condensation on the outside showing it was cold. The beer was a light golden colour and had tiny bubbles rising from the bottom of the glass and around the top was a white head about ten millimetres deep.

He picked it up and took a sip. Carina was watching him intently for a reaction. Datch savoured the beer for a moment and smiled.

"This isn't bad. I could take a liking to this." He said and took a big gulp.

They all took a drink and looked around at the bar. It was about half the size of the Barbers Inn on Bellatrix and had been divided into two sections. One side was for food and had tables laid out with cutlery and various condiments similar to a restaurant. The other side was the main bar with tall tables with stools around them. It also had a couple of TV screens displaying one of the sports channels that was showing something called baseball. In the centre of the bar area was a table with holes in the corners that Kristina said was a pool table.

They sat looking around the bar and trying to understand how the humans behaved to each other. They were just about to order their second round of drinks when the food came out. Datch looked at his plate. The steak was huge and came with chips, mushrooms, a large red thing cut in two and grilled. According to Kristina it was called a 'tomato', also, it came with a salad that consisted of some green leafy stuff.

Datch waited until the waitress had gone and carefully pulled out his hand scanner. He scanned the food making sure that no one could see him and then checked the results.

'It's good to eat.' came Datch's voice in Carina's head.

Down the street a van pulled up outside the bank and two security men got out with another man wearing an engineer's suit. They walked over to the ATM and the engineer looked at it. After a few moments he pressed a few buttons and then put a card in the slot. He pressed a few more buttons but had a puzzled look on his face. He pressed some more and then tried again. Still the same thing. He got out his mobile phone and made a call.

The bank manager was sitting eating dinner with his wife when his phone rang. He picked it up and answered it.

"Hello?"

"Am I speaking to Mr Jacobs?"

"Yes."

"I'm Paul from ATM services. We came to look at a fault on the machine outside your bank. When we got here it had been emptied."

"What? Didn't you fill it earlier?"

"Yes, we did but it's been emptied without any sign of the money being withdrawn."

"Are you sure?"

"Yes, it is only listing twenty or so transaction of less than two hundred dollars each but the machine is totally empty."

"What all of it?"

"Yes, as far as I can tell, twenty-one thousand dollars has been taken."

"Oh no, not again."

"Again?"

"Yes, it happened a few months ago and no one knew how they did it. Anyway, I'm on my way down to the bank."

"Sir, I've got to call the police now to report the missing money."

"Ok. I will see you there shortly."

The bank manger picked his jacket up and after telling his wife what was going on, headed out the door in a hurry.

An hour later Datch sat looking at what was left of his plate. The steak had been quite large and he was stuffed. He also had drunk three beers that weren't helping the size of his stomach. *'Hmm'* he thought, *'Maybe the red thing was a bit too much.'*

'Very likely.' Came a second voice in his head.

'What did you think?' He thought.

'It was very nice.' Came back the voice.

"Are we having sweets?" Asked Kristina.

"Yes, why not?" Said Datch not wanting to be out done by a human.

'Really?' Said the voice.

'Yes.'

"Ok, looks like they have a chocolate ice-cream sundae, that sounds good."

"Yes, I'll have one of them as well," added Carina.

"Me too." Said Kristina.

Datch waved at the waitress and she came over.

"Can we please have three chocolate ice-cream sundaes?"

"Sure, no problem."

She headed off to fetch them and five minutes later came back with them.

Datch sat looking at his. If it had been possible his eyes would have been out on storks. He lifted his spoon and pick a piece up, carefully placing it in his mouth. His face was a picture of happiness and joy as the chocolate Ice-cream melted in his mouth.

"Oh my." He said, "this is amazing."

He shoved a large spoon full in his mouth forgetting all about his stomach being full.

The girls started to tuck into theirs. Datch recorded what the sundae was like and how it was put together with his implant.

"We need these back at home." he said with his mouth full.

"I'll second that." Said Carina.

Down the street the bank manager was showing the police the CCTV recording from outside the bank. They watched as two bikes drove into the car park and one of the riders got off. The biker walked over to the ATM and after a few moments started putting money into a bag. Then he turned and got back on his bike and drove off followed by the other bike. For some reason the camera was finding it hard to focus on the person and they couldn't make out their face no matter how they looked at the recording. The same was true for any details of the bikes and other riders.

"Well, the bikes shouldn't be hard to find. Looks like they have them ready for a carnival. I'll put out an all-points bulletin for them."

"Thank you, officer." Said the bank manager.

"We'll need a copy of the CCTV footage. I'll see if our experts can improve the image any."

"Certainly, I'll back it up now for you."

Down the street Datch, Carina and Kristina paid their bill and left a nice tip for the waitress before getting up and heading for the door. They went outside into the warm evening air and climbed onto the bikes.

"Let's head back to the Raven and have a nap." Said Datch.

"OK, sounds good, that steak was very filling."

They started the bikes up and pulled out of the parking lot. They headed back down the street towards the bank and the road they had used to come into the city.

There were a couple of police cars outside the bank with an officer standing having a cigarette. He looked at them as they came down the road and shouted through the door. Another officer ran out the door and looked at them. He shouted "Stop!".

"Err, looks like they have spotted us. Let's move it." said Datch.

"Ok, switching limiters off." Said Carina.

They started to accelerate down the street. The police jumped in their car and started to chase after them.

"This is car 68 in pursuit of two bikes believed to be involved in an ATM theft. We are heading down 74th street. Requesting assistance over."

"Copy that car 68. Car 41 will assist."

Datch increased speed to a hundred and twenty KPH but the police car was in hot pursuit. They reached a junction and another police car joined in.

"I think we need to go up and then to full thrust. Lock on to the Raven." Said Datch who was quite enjoying the fun.

"OK, I've locked on to the Raven with my nav system." said Carina.

The two police cars were right behind them with their sirens wailing and lights flashing.

"Ok, Let's do it." said Datch.

He increased the power control to max and pulled back on the handle bars. The bikes took to the air flying up above the street and buildings leaving the police cars behind as if they had been standing still. Datch turned the bike to the right and they disappeared over a building and into the darkness of the sky.

The two police cars slowed down and stopped. One officer turned to the other.

"So, how do we report that?"

"Hmm… I have no idea. But I think we should go to the donut shop first. I need a sugar fix." Said the other.

Datch lined the bike up on the nav systems line and the bikes thundered across the night sky. The farmer that had come out earlier picked up his phone and called the airbase to complain about their pilots flying low at night as it was disturbing his animals and more to the point the program he was trying to watch on the TV.

They started to get close to the Raven and Datch slowed down and Carina followed suit. Up ahead were the trees hiding the Raven. Datch dropped the bike down to just above the ground and pressed a button on the console.

As they approached the ramp dropped down and the cargo bay door opened. Datch flew the bike straight in and touched down in the cargo bay. Carina followed behind him and landed next to him. They shut the bikes down and dismounted.

"Well, that was fun." Said Datch grinning.

"Fun?" Asked Kristina.

"Yes." Said Datch.

"We got chased by the police. We could have got caught."

"Not a chance. They can't fly and we could have easily out run them."

"Yes, but they now know what the bikes look like now." Said Carina.

"Oh, Good point. Still, we don't need them again."

"So, how are we getting into LA then?" Said Kristina.

"We're taking the Raven."

"You're going to fly the Raven into the middle of LA?"

"Yes, I have a plan."

"I need a drink." Said Kristina.

Carina just stood there smiling, Datch loved the dramatic and he was in his element now.

"Let's go and have another beer before we get some sleep. We need to get up earlier as we need to get there before it gets too busy."

Kristina just looked at him.

'You do realise she is worried.' Came Carina's voice in his head.

'Yes, but we're having fun.'

'So, what is the plan?'

'We need to make a sign with Centaurs Movie Company on it'

'We do?'

'Yes, and another that says Star Warrior on it.'

"Err… are you two doing that mind thing again?" asked Kristina who was standing looking at them.

"Oh, Sorry, we were just going over the plan." Said Datch.

"And that is?"

"Now you wouldn't want me to spoil all the fun would you."

"Yes!"

"Well, I'm not going to." He looked at Carina.

"It's no good Kristina. Datch won't tell you until he's ready. That's what he does." Added Carina.

They sat having a drink and watching another program about LA on the vid before heading to bed.

Los Angeles

Datch woke up to the alarm going off. He jumped out of bed only to realise it was his wakeup alarm. Carina stirred and looked at him.

"What's up?" She asked.

"Nothing, it was the alarm for us to get up."

"O…K… Get me a coffee. I'll have a shower and then wake Kristina." said Carina yawning.

"OK." Datch said and went for a quick shower first.

Carina went and woke Kristina while Datch finished his shower and while Carina was having hers, he sorted out three coffees in the rec room. He was just sitting down when they both came in.

"I need to have a look at a street plan of LA before anything else." said Datch.

"Ok." said Carina hoping for a clue or two about what they were about to do.

"Computer please display all the ice-cream parlours in Los Angeles on a map of the city."

The computer displayed a map of the city and overlayed the ice-cream shops on the map.

"Now show all the tall buildings that could interfere with flight paths into the city."

The computer highlighted a number of buildings in red and placed numbers on the top indicating their height in metres.

"Hmm. OK now display parking areas that would be able to take the ships size."

Carina and Kristina both turned to look at Datch.

"You're not thinking of taking the Raven into LA and just parking it, are you?" asked Carina in disbelief.

"Err, yes. that's what I needed the signs for."

"They will see you." said Kristina.

"Yes, They will. I'm counting on it. Where is the best place to hide something?" Asked Datch.

"I don't know, I've never been to LA." Said Kristina.

"That's not what I meant. The best place to hide something is in plain sight." Said Datch.

"You're telling me you're going to park an alien space ship in the middle of LA and no one will notice?" Asked Kristina.

"Well, no, they will see it, they may even take pictures of it and the media might even put it on the news but it will not cause unwanted attention."

"Why wouldn't it?" asked Carina who was starting to think Datch had lost the plot.

"Because they will think it's normal." He said grinning.

"I know that look." Said Carina looking at him.

"You do?" Asked Kristina.

"Yes. It means things are going to get interesting."

"Interesting?"

"Yes." said Datch. He turned back to the computer.

"Computer please give me a parking lot near to an Ice-cream Parlour."

The computer showed three ice-cream parlours with routes from parking lots.

"That one looks good. Ice Tastic, it says they have a large variety of flavours."

"And we're just going to fly in?"

"Yes, trust me this will be fun. Let's finish our coffee and head to the cockpit. We need to get there around dawn which is in about forty minutes earth time."

"I hope this works." said Carina.

"It will. Computer, please replicate the signs I designed. I'll collect them from the reactor room in a bit."

They finished their coffees and headed to the cockpit. Datch went through the pre-flight checks and started checking for traffic in local area.

"Ok, Everyone ready?"

"No." Said Kristina, "But I take it we're going anyway."

"Yes."

Datch brought the engines online and the Raven took to the sky. The flight took about twenty minutes and Datch was flying high again to avoid any unwanted contacts with any other air traffic.

Dawn was just breaking as the Raven started its descent towards the city. Below, most of the city was still in shadow as the sun slowly came above the horizon. Most of the street lights were still on and there was not very much traffic on the roads. Datch slowed the Raven as it descended. In his head display he could see the other aircraft and the airport was busy. He brought the Raven down toward the skyscrapers and clear air. The Raven had its scattering field running so the radar systems could not detect them and the only chance of being spotted was if a pilot of one of aircraft happened to look at them. Datch flew the Raven low over one of the streets. Halfway down the street was a parking lot. He turned the ship and brought the Raven in for a landing in the front part of it near street.

"Now what?" said Carina.

"We go and get the signs and talk to that man over there before he calls the police." Said Datch getting up.

They walked down to the cargo bay collecting the very big signs on the way.

The parking attendant looked at what had just landed in his lot. It didn't look like a helicopter but it landed like one and it wasn't like any other aircraft he knew of. Maybe I should call someone he thought. He was just about to pick up his phone when the rear of the craft opened and three people wearing sun glasses came walking down carrying some signs. He left his booth and headed over to meet them.

"Hey, you can't park that there." He said waving at the Raven.

Datch walked up to him.

"Hello. I'm Datch from the Centaurs Movie Company. I would like to give you the easiest days work in your life and make it worth your while as well."

The man looked at him, then at the Raven, then at the girls who were both smiling and then back at Datch.

"Easy, in what way?"

"Well, we want to put up some signs to advertise our new movie called Star Warrior. The Helicopter behind me has been made up to look like the space ship in the movie and hopefully will stir up interest. Of course, we will make it worth your while and it will only be here for one day. How much does you parking lot take in a day?"

"Err, well about five thousand dollars." Replied the man

"Well, if we gave you say eight thousand dollars for parking it here and say another two thousand for yourself after all it is causing you trouble. How would that sound?"

The man looked at him and thought about it.

"And it will only be here for a day?"

"Yes, it will be gone by the morning."

"Hmm. Maybe I could let you park here but it would have to be cash."

"Oh yes, we thought you would say that. We have it in twenty dollar bills. All we ask is that you don't let anyone go touching it. It is a movie prop after all."

The man decided that the two thousand dollars would come in very handy not to mention the bragging rights in his local bar later.

"Oh, yes. No problem, Sir. Do you need a hand with anything?"

"Err… you don't happen to have anything we can put around it do you?"

"Well, not all the way but I have some plastic bollards and barriers we use. They should work."

"Great, that sounds good. You get them and I'll get your money."

"Ok."

The man headed off to a shed in the corner of the lot. Datch walked back to the girls.

"Well?" Asked Carina.

"Yep, we're good to park here. Start putting the signs up and make sure they are very visible. I'm going to get the man his money."

"You're telling me we have just landed a space ship in a man's parking lot and he's happy for us to park it here?"

"Yes. Back in a minute." Said Datch grinning.

He headed inside the Raven.

The man came over carrying a number of plastic barriers.

"Good morning, ladies." He said as he walked up.

"Good morning." Said Carina,

"Hola." Said Kristina.

"I'll put these across here if it's, ok?" he said.

"Sure, sounds good." said Carina.

He started setting up the barriers while Carina and Kristina put the signs up.

"I must say, you have made it look very realistic." he said.

"Yes, it took a long time and a lot of work." said Carina.

"You would never guess there was a helicopter inside."

'Helicopter?' came a voice in Datch's head.

'Oh, yes he thinks it's a helicopter made to look like a space ship. sorry forgot to tell you.'

Carina turned to the man.

"Yes, they did a very good job of hiding it."

Just then Datch came walking back down the ramp with two bags in his hands and walked over to the attendant who was just finishing putting another barrier up.

"Here you are sir. This Bag has the eight thousand for the parking fee and this one has the extra two thousand for you. Thank you again for all you're help."

"You're welcome. Are you going to be stopping here all day?"

"No. We have some business meetings to go to. You know deals and stuff. You don't happen to know anywhere we can get something for breakfast?"

"Yes, there's a good diner down the street over there that does breakfast."

"Ok, Thanks."

He helped the man set up the rest of the barriers and they stood back and looked at their handy work.

The Raven stood surrounded by barriers with two big signs in front of it. One said 'Star Warrior coming soon.' And the other said 'from the Centaurs Movie Company.' It looked like part of a movie lot instead of a parking lot.

"Could you take a picture of me in front of it please?"

"Sure."

The man handed him his phone. Datch looked at it slightly puzzled. Kristina spotted Datch and went over. She whispered in his ear.

"You two go each side of him and I'll take the picture."

"Thanks. This device is a little primitive."

"Carina, let's stand with him and have the picture. Kristina is going to take it."

They stood either side of the man and smiled at Kristina. She pressed the phone and the flash went off. To make sure she took a second one.

"There you go. Just remember it's Carina and Datch." Said Datch.

"Thank you. I will." Said the man and wished them a good day before heading back to his booth to count the money and call his friends.

The three of them went back inside Raven where they picked up a rucksack each and Datch collected the rest of the money.

"Are we taking the bikes?"

"No, but put one of our personal shields on."

Carina stopped for a moment.

"Why?"

"You watched the vid. People shot people in the city. It's best to be safe and no one will see them."

"OK. I'll fit one to Kristina too."

"One what?" said Kristina walking over.

"It's a personal shield. It will stop anyone knifing or shooting you."

"Cool. How does it work?"

"The same way as the ships shields did in the jungle."

"Oh. OK then."

Carina helped attach the little unit to Kristina's waist. And then did her own.

"Right, let's go and see LA."

"Breakfast first, right?" said Kristina who was hungry.

"Yes, breakfast." said Datch.

They walked down the ramp and closed it behind them.

"Will it be, ok?" Asked Carina looking at the Raven.

"Yes. I have the ship's systems linked to my vid com so I'll know if there is a problem." Said Datch.

"OK."

They waved at the man in his booth. He was on his phone but put his hand up to them. He had put a barrier across the entrance to stop any cars turning in with a sign on it saying 'SORRY – WE ARE FULL'

They headed down the street. The traffic was picking up a bit now. The sun was up and it was a lovely morning. The sun was warm and you didn't sweat buckets as you walked down the road unlike in the jungle.

They spotted the diner. It was the ground floor of a four-story building and had a neon lighting above it saying 'Sally's'. They crossed the street and headed inside. The room was laid out with tables and chairs running down both sides and a counter at the far end. Above the counter were three TV screens displaying the current menu. They looked at them. It took the implants a few seconds but then it became readable. Then Carina spotted them.

"Do you want pancakes?" She asked.

"Yes, please." Said Datch.

"What about you, Kristina?"

"Yes, sounds good."

Across the city three men sat looking at a strange piece of equipment.

"Are you sure?"

"Yes, only for a moment though. It was a short burst."

"Did you get a fix?"

"Only a rough one. It was in a ten block radius."

"Ok, that will have to do. Can we use the portable equipment when we get there?"

"Yes, but it's not very sensitive, we'll have to be very close as the signal strength is so small."

"Tim, you stay here and contact us if the signal appears again. OK, Jay, let's go."

Jay picked up a bag and two of them left the room.

Datch sat looking at the pancakes. Each of them had a stack of them in front of them. Each stack had chocolate syrup dripping of it.

"Are you going to sit looking at it all day?" Asked Kristina.

"Oh… sorry, no," said Carina.

They all started eating.

"These are good pancakes." Said Datch with his mouth full.

"Yes." Carina managed between bites.

They sat and munched their way through the pile of food and then washed it down with some coffee.

"That was good, so what we doing now?" asked Carina taking her last sip of coffee.

"Well, it looks like the ice cream parlours don't open till lunch time so I thought a bit of sightseeing would be a nice idea. We are here on holiday after all." Said Datch.

"Ok, where to then?"

"Let's start with a walk around the centre of the city and then head across to Venice beach. We could go for a paddle while we're there."

"Sounds good."

Datch asked his implant for the route to the city centre. It came back with a route but it was about six kilometres.

They finished their coffees and left the diner. Datch stopped at a bus stop.

"I think this may get us there quicker." he said.

He worked out that they needed a number twelve bus which went to the city centre. They stood waiting at the bus stop. Five minutes later a bus came down the street and lucky for them it was a number twelve.

They got onboard and paid the driver before heading up stairs so they could get a better view. The bus pulled off and started to head into the city. They sat looking at all the buildings and people heading to work. The scene was new to them as rush hours didn't exist on Bellatrix five. At home people who were able to work from home did and everyone else did hours that suited them. The result of which was that the streets were never overly busy. The three of them relaxed and watched the city go by outside.

A blue car with two men in passed the bus heading the opposite way. The man sitting in the passenger seat was looking at a piece of equipment in his hand when his phone rang.

"Yes?" he said.

"Are you sure?"

"Ok." he hung up.

"He's just picked up another signal same area. Hey what's going on there."

They pulled the car over to the side of the road. There was a small group of people taking photos which was odd for 9am. They got out and headed over to the crowd. They were taking photos of what looked like a space ship but it had barriers around it and a number of signs in front of it. The man with the piece of equipment pointed it at the Raven.

"Hmm. It's not giving off any signals that I can pick up."

"I'll go ask what it is to be sure."

The man who had been driving walked over to the booth where an attendant was standing.

"Excuse me, what is that?"

"Oh, it's from a new movie. They landed here this morning."

"Landed it?"

"Yes, it's got a helicopter inside."

"Oh, could I have a look?"

"You can't stand under it as it might not be safe but for five dollars you can stand in front of it and I'll take your photo for you."

"Ok, Thanks but I'm good. You don't happen to know where the people from it went do you?"

The man looked at him and waited.

"Ok, here." he gave him five dollars.

"They went down the street over there for breakfast."

"Did they say they were coming back?"

He waited again and then another five dollars was handed over.

"They said, they had a few business meetings to go to and wouldn't be back till tonight. That's all I know."

"Oh, OK. thank you."

The man turned and went back to the other one.

"Well?"

"There is a helicopter inside it apparently and the people who came with it have gone off into the city somewhere."

"OK, you could get a helicopter in there but where would the air come down to give it lift. The bottom looks solid."

"Well, the man over there is not letting anyone close to it and says it's not safe."

"Hmm, I wonder." Just then his phone rang.

"Hello?"

"What, near the centre?"

"OK, Thanks."

"We just picked up another signal near the city centre. Let's head there. If that is a space ship it's not giving off any signals that I can detect."

They got back in their car and headed towards the city centre.

Datch, Carina and Kristina got off the bus and headed in the direction of a market. It was listed on a tourist map that Datch had found stuffed in the back of his seat on the bus. The morning sun was now getting quite strong as It was going up for ten am by this time.

The market was laid out with stalls running down both sides and also in the centre forming a number of aisles that ran the full length of the building. There were stalls with fruit and vegetables, fish stalls, meat stalls, one's with fresh pastries and cakes, others had sugary sweets and candyfloss. Some were selling cooking implements and electrical appliances while others had souvenirs and hand-crafted items on them. The market was full of different smells and humans who were busy buying all sorts of things.

"Wow, this place is busy." Said Carina.

"Yes, and look at all this great stuff." Said Datch looking at one of the stalls.

"Maybe we should get some gifts for the others."

"Sounds good. Let's see what we can find for them."

"What about your mum and dad?"

"Ah…" Datch thought about this for a moment, they weren't really meant to be on Earth. He then remembered that his dad had been here.

"Ok, Let's look for something cool for them."

"Others?" Asked Kristina.

"Yes, our friends."

Kristina suddenly realised they were talking about their friends on another planet. She had thought of them as just two aliens and now it hit her that there was a lot more of them.

"I never thought of it till now but there are lots of you, aren't there?"

Datch picked up a model of one of the buildings.

"Yes, six galaxies full." He said without thinking.

"Six galaxies full!" Said Kristina.

Datch realised what he had said.

"Err, you didn't hear that." He said hoping she might forget it.

She stood looking at him.

"I did."

"Err, well try to forget it please. We're not meant to say anything. It could sort of change your outlook on the universe."

"OK. One, I've been on your space ship. Two, I can speak your language and Three, I'm over six thousand kilometres away from where I should have died four days ago."

"Ah well, err, just keep it to yourself please." Said Datch trying to work out what to say.

"What, Datch is trying to say is, please remember if the population of Earth found out about us now the entire planet's population would go into shock which could cause irreparable damage to your planet's culture not to mention that the planet is very war like at the moment and as such would likely get itself quarantined from the rest of the galaxy." said Carina.

"Yes. Earth's not ready yet," added Datch.

"So, I'm just meant to keep quiet?" Asked Kristina.

"Sorry, but yes. Still, we'll drop you back in Brazil before we leave."

"I wanted to see space though."

"I'll take you there on the way back, ok?"

"OK."

"Right, do you think my mum would like this?" said Datch changing the subject and holding up a wooden carving of the city hall.

"Yes, it will look nice in their lounge."

"What about this for Tank?" said Carina holding up a pink fluffy dolphin.

"Yes, he'll like that."

They came to a food stall selling snacks. Datch looked at them and then had to ask his implant what they were. The Ravens computer was scanning the internet and finding the answers for them. After the implant had responded he picked up a couple of packets of sweets and a box of chocolates.

They moved a bit further down the market picking this and that up.

"What do you think about this for Clax." said Datch lifting up a book that was about ancient Egypt with lots of picture's in."

"Yes, he would love that. Look here…" said Carina pointing to a heated boot warmer.

"Fred!" said Datch.

And they both laughed.

"Err, what?"

"Don't worry, it's a long story."

They reach the other side of the market and sat down at a café to have a drink.

"Hmm, we should get something for Jim as well."

"Yes, I have an idea for that but I can't see anything here."

"Maybe down there a bit?" said Carina pointing down the road.

Datch looked at his vid com and then down the street.

"Looks like a shopping mall down there. I think it's a good bet."

The two men in the car were parked outside a department store looking around at the people in the street.

The man's phone rang again.

"Hello."

"Ok, the market area. We're on our way."

He turned to the man next to him.

"Head to the market. There was another signal pulse."

They headed off towards the market.

Datch, Carina and Kristina finished their drinks and headed down the street. After a couple of blocks, they found a big shopping mall and headed in through the doors.

"So, what were you thinking?"

"What about…" he looked into space for a moment. "a tankard." He showed an image of it to them on his vid com.

"Yes, he'd like that."

"That will be either in a jewellery store or novelty shop depending what you want." Asked Kristina.

"Err, maybe a fancy one?"

"Ok, Jewellery store then."

The mall had all sorts of shops, food stores, clothing stores, technology shops and jewellers.

They found one on the second floor that had some tankards and the woman was more than happy to show them what she had. There were about twenty different ones. Some were very fancy while others were quite plain in their design. They decided that a plain one was a good idea and went for a pewter one as it looked, well, Earth like. Datch did a very quick and subtle scan with his handheld scanner to check it was safe and then they bought it.

The shop assistant noticed him.

"Err, can I ask what you doing?"

Datch had to think fast.

"Oh, this is linked to my phone so we can tick things off our gift list."

"Wow, that's cool, where did you get it?"

Datch was thinking hard again but this time Carina beat him.

"We got it from China." She said.

"Typical, everything comes from China these days." Said the shop assistant with a sigh.

She wrapped up the tankard for them and Datch put it in his now full looking rucksack.

The two men were just walking into the market when their phone rang.

"Hello." He said.

The man standing next to him couldn't hear the man on the other end of the phone, only what his partner was saying.

"Yes, we just got to the market."

"What?"

"Can't you do something to get us a better fix?"

"I know the equipment is not the best but that was all we were able to build."

"Yes, but you know the rules."

"No. Just try to tell us before we park up."

"Ok, yes it's good you have it down to a city block."

"What? The mall?"

"Ok, we're on our way."

He ended the call.

"They are in the shopping mall; well, they were about five minutes ago anyway."

"So, what do we do?"

"You go back and fetch the car and I'll go on foot. Call me when you get there, ok?"

"OK."

One of the men headed back to the car park while the other headed across the market and out of the door on the opposite side.

Datch looked around.

"I want to get Jep a book about Earth. I think he would enjoy it. Hmm, But I don't see any in here."

"No. me neither." Said Carina.

Datch got out his vid com and did a search for bookshops. After a few moments it beeped and displayed a map of the city with the bookshops and their current position.

"Ok, this way. There is one a couple of blocks away." He said and they headed outside.

As they came out the door a man went running in looking out of breath. They turned and headed down the street.

In the man's pocket something went beep. He stopped and looked at it and then looked around at all the people. They all looked normal and were busy going about their own business and that was shopping. He took the device out of his pocket and looked at it. It had picked up a signal that was within a few metres but it had gone now. He sighed and then his phone rang.

"Yes, I'm just inside the main doors."

He hung up and went to sit on a seat near one of the shops where he could watch the doors. A woman came over to him.

"Good morning, what can I get you?" She asked.

The man looked around and then realised he was sitting outside a café.

"Oh, err, can I have two regular coffees please?"

"Sure."

"Thanks."

He sat and waited while watching the area looking for anyone who didn't fit. Two minutes later a man came walking through the door. He waved at him and he came over and sat down.

"Well?"

"I picked up a signal as I came into the mall. It was within a few metres but I couldn't get a fix. I'm trying to spot who it came from but so far nothing."

"So, what's the plan?"

"Coffee. I need a drink and we can watch the doors from here."

"OK, sounds good."

Datch, Carina and Kristina found the bookshop and went in. There were a lot of books and Datch stood looking at the room. They didn't have bookshops on Bellatrix as everyone had access to everything just by downloading it to their vid coms or using their implants.

"So, what we looking for?" Asked Carina.

"I think something with nice pictures and information about the planet." Said Datch.

"You want an encyclopaedia." Said Kristina.

"An encyclopaedia? OK, what do they look like?" Asked Datch.

"I don't know. They have all sorts of different covers." Said Kristina.

"Oh..."

"I'll ask." said Carina.

She went over to the shop assistant and asked her if they had any. She took them over to a shelf at the back.

"These are all encyclopaedias; you should find what you're looking for here." Said the assistant.

"OK, thank you."

They stood looking at the books. It took a few minutes but they found a medium sized one with pictures and details about the planet in general. They paid for it and went outside.

"OK. Where now?" asked Kristina.

"The beach and then ice cream." said Datch grinning.

He checked his vid com for buses going to the beach and found a stop not far away.

"This way." he said and they headed off to find the bus stop.

The two men sat watching the people leaving the mall and drinking their coffees. The man's phone rang again.

"Hello."

"Oh! OK."

He hung up.

"They are not here. He's picked another signal a couple of blocks away."

"Let's go then."

"No. Let's finish our coffees. They won't be there when we get there. I wish I knew where they were going?"

"Well, it looks like they are doing a bit of shopping and sightseeing."

"Yes, I gathered that. We are sitting in a mall. But how does that help us?"

"Well, if that is their ship back at the parking lot, they will be wanting to take their shopping back soon."

"Good thinking. After the coffees we'll head back and wait for them."

The bus ride was a nice relaxing trip with a number of interesting sights to look at on the route. It took about thirty minutes to get to the beach. The bus stop was on the sea front and the three of them got off.

The beach was very long and had a path that ran along the back of it with joggers running along it. There was also an outdoor gym with people working out in the sunshine using weights and various other pieces of gym equipment. Most of them were trying to look cool and failing to do so due to the sweat pouring off of them.

The beach itself was busy with people sunbathing on the sunbeds and others were laying on towels placed on the sand. The sea was lapping gently on the shore and was full of people swimming and splashing about. Further out jet skies were racing about along with other pleasure craft. Datch watched a jet ski come by and thought it looked fun.

They found a patch of sand a couple of metres from the water. Carina reached in her bag and got out a beach blanket that she had bought from one of the shops in the mall. She had also got two towels which she put on the blanket.

"Wow!" said Kristina sitting down. "I've never seen the sea before."

"You haven't?" Asked Carina.

"No, jungle and cities only. It was one place I always wanted to go but never thought I would get the chance."

"Well, you're getting to see a lot of things now." Said Datch.

"Yes, thanks again." Kristina looked at the sea. "I never thought the sea was so big." She added.

"Talking of sea. I'm going to cool my feet off." Datch said.

He took his shoes off and headed for the water.

"Hey, wait for me." Said Carina.

They all got up and headed to the water. They stood up to their knees in water cooling off. The sun was hot and the water was warm.

They spent the next two hours on the beach then Datch decided it was time for ice cream. He pulled out his vid com and looked for the easiest way to get to 'Ice Tastic' ice cream parlour. After a couple of minutes, he came to a conclusion.

"I think we need to get a taxi back to the ice-cream parlour. It looks like we would have to take at least two different buses to get there so it would be a lot quicker."

"Ok, let's get our things together."

They picked up the blanket and towels and put them back in Carina's bag before walking up the beach back to where the bus had dropped them off.

Datch looked at his vid com again and found that the taxi rank was a bit further down the beach. They headed down the road to it and found a taxi. Datch told him where they were going and they got in. It reminded Datch of Arcaneus when they went to the spaceport with all its knobs and a steering wheel.

The two men were sitting across the road from the parking lot reading a paper and watching the Raven. It was quite busy with a lot of people standing looking at it. There was even a film crew from one of the news channels hoping to catch the company representatives and find out more about the film.

"A thought has just crossed my mind?"

"What?"

"Well, if they are aliens then how are we going to separate them from the crowd without causing it to be on the six o'clock news?"

"Hmm. That is a bit of a problem. If they are aliens then the population must not know."

The two men looked across the street and sighed.

Then one of the men's phones started ringing. He got it out and looked at it.

"Hello."

"The beach!"

"Right, we'll go and have lunch."

He ended the call.

"They're at the beach. Most likely having a paddle with our luck."

"Oh."

"We might as well go have lunch."

They got up and headed to the street where the diner was.

The taxi headed across the city taking three quarters of an hour to get there. The taxi slowed down and stopped outside a large shop. It had a sign with two large ice cream cones on and in the middle were the words 'Ice Tastic'.

Datch paid the driver and they got out. He stood looking at the shop. There was another large sign stating that they have thirty-five different flavours of ice cream inside and then listed a long list of ice cream dishes that they would make for you.

"Are you standing outside or going in?" asked Carina with a slight bit of sarcasm in her voice.

"Oh, yes," said Datch snapping out of a trance.

The three of them walked inside the shop.

The shop was decorated in light pinks and blues with pictures of ice cream dishes on the walls. It was laid out with seating in front of the windows and on the opposite side was a long-refrigerated counter. Datch went over to it. The ice cream was in metal trays and set out in colourful groups. Datch's eyes were like saucers and he was drooling out the side of his mouth which was not a good look for him. There were flavours like rum and raisin, mint and chocolate chip, not to mention the mid-west whisky and pecans. Datch had a very big smile on his face that was likely to make the top of his head fall off if it got much bigger.

"So, what would you like?" Asked Carina.

"Err… I don't know." he said looking very confused and worried at the same time.

"Well, pick one."

The assistant came over.

"I'm not sure what to pick, I like the sound of the rum and raisin, the blueberry and also the dark chocolate truffle."

"Sir, I can do a scoop of each and put them in a bowl for you."

"Can you? That would be fantastic, thanks." Datch's smile was so big he could have swallowed his own ears.

The assistant took a large scoop of each and put them in a polystyrene bowl with a plastic spoon.

Carina then picked three herself and finally it was Kristina's turn and she did the same.

They paid the assistant and went and sat down.

"This looks so good. Let me scan it."

He got out his scanner that sort of looked like a small chunky phone and scanned each of the lumps of ice cream.

"What are you doing?" Asked Kristina

"I'm recording the molecular makeup of the ice cream. Hopefully the people at the ice cream plant on Bellatrix can make copies of it."

"You can do that?"

"Yes, I just need to be careful not to mix the flavours."

"Oh, cool."

Datch finished scanning his and passed the scanner to Carina who did the same with hers.

"Do you want to do mine as well?" Asked Kristina.

"Yes, that would be great thanks."

She pointed the scanner at her bowl and scanned each of the scoops each time asking what it was.

"Right, that's nine out of the thirty-five." said Datch and tucked into his bowl with a look of someone who really meant business.

Kristina watched in disbelief as Datch devoured the ice cream like he hadn't eaten for a month. The bowl didn't last long.

"Wow, you finished that off fast."

"Yes, I need more."

Carina was on her second scoop and only took a couple of minutes. Kristina was just starting her second scoop when they stood up.

"Carina, let's get some more."

"Ok."

"Err, guys, I don't eat that fast and I think I'll be full after these."

"Ok."

Carina and Datch went back to the counter and picked three more each. The assistant looked at them as they went back to the table. Datch again went to scan them but halfway through the scanner beeped.

He looked at it. The small screen was showing a brain symbol with an X over it.

"What's up?" asked Carina.

"The memory is full. I'll have to download it to the Raven."

He fetched out his Vid com and connected it to the scanner. He pressed a couple of buttons and the scanner downloaded the data to the Raven's storage.

"Ok, We're good."

He carried on scanning his ice cream and then handed the scanner to Carina.

The two men had finished lunch and were back sitting on the seat opposite the parking lot.

The man's phone rang again.

"Hello."

"You did? Great, Where?"

"In a laundry, ice cream parlour or coffee shop?"

"Ok, Where?"

"Ok, we're on our way."

He hung up the phone.

"He just picked up a longer signal burst and got a good fix on their position. It's two blocks away in one of three shops, a laundry, an ice cream shop or a café, so let's go."

They got up and went walking up the road. They left the car as it would take longer to fetch it than walk the two blocks.

Datch and Carina finished off their bowls all be it a little slower this time and Kristina was just finishing hers when they got up and went to the counter again.

The shop assistant looked at them. If they carried on going, she could see herself having to do some mopping up in the near future and this time it wouldn't be the kids that had too much.

"You know we sell take outs, don't you?" she asked.

"Take outs?"

"Yes, we sell tubs you can take way with you for later."

"Oh. OK. Can I have one of each of the one's we haven't had yet please. In fact, make that one of all the flavours in the shop?"

"Are you sure? That's about two hundred and fifty bucks' worth of ice cream."

"Yes, please and do you have a couple of bags to put them in?"

"Yes, and you really want one carton of each?"

"Yes."

"And you can pay?"

"Yes."

Datch showed her a hand full of twenty dollar bills.

"Ok…then."

She turned and went into the walking freezer at the back and started filling bags with cartons of ice cream. It took a couple of minutes before she came out carrying three large bags full of cartons. She went to the cash register and rang them in. The total cost came to two hundred and sixty-eight dollars eighty cents. Datch handed her two hundred and eighty dollars and told her to keep the change.

They walked over to Kristina.

"What have you got?"

"Take outs." Said Datch grinning.

"Well, we had better get them back before they melt."

"Ah, yes. good point. Let's make a move."

Outside the two men decided to check the café first and went inside it just as Datch, Carina and Kristina came out of the ice cream parlour looking a little over loaded. Each of

them had three bags except for Datch and Carina who also
had large rucksacks on their backs.

The three of them headed off to the parking lot. They
quickened the pace so the ice cream didn't melt. When they
arrived at the parking lot, there were a group of people
outside on the sidewalk and a tv crew who appeared to be
having a coffee break.

Datch went and tapped the attendant on his shoulder and
he turned around.

"Oh, Hello."

"Hi, how's it going?"

"Very well indeed. There's a number of people from the
press who want to know about the film?"

"Hmm, we can't say anything at the moment. Deals and
things you know?"

"Oh yes, I understand."

"Cool, Err, we want to put our bags inside and if possible,
without being seen."

"I have just the thing."

He looked at Datch and waited.

Datch got out a ten-dollar bill and gave it to him. He
smiled and reached inside his booth and fetched out three
high vis vests and a clipboard with a pen attached.

"What about them?" said Datch looking at the news crew.

"I'll tell them you're parking inspectors and they had better
check their parking meter."

"Ok."

Two minutes later they walked under the Raven dressed in bright vests and headed to the back out of sight of the crowd. Datch dropped the ramp down and they went inside.

A member of the news crew came over to the attendant.

"Who are they?"

"Who them?"

"Yes."

"They are inspectors from city hall, they want to make sure it's safe."

"Oh."

"Oh, and make sure your truck has the meter full."

"Ah yes. good point."

He went back to the rest of the crew and shouted at someone to put money in the parking meter.

Inside the Raven, the three of them headed to the storeroom and put the ice cream in stasis section so it wouldn't melt anymore then Kristina helped them put the gifts away.

"So, what now?" Asked Carina.

"Well, I think we should freshen up and then go for a beer. I don't want to move the Raven until dark." said Datch.

"Ok, I could do with a shower." said Carina.

"Me too." said Kristina.

The girls went off to get freshened up.

Trouble in LA

An hour later they sat in the rec room. Datch had put the external monitors up on the vid and was watching the crowd outside. There were no signs of anything untoward and members of the crowd would take a few photos before wandering off and some more people would take their place.

"Datch, why don't we find a bar with food? After all, this will be our last chance to eat here." Said Carina.

"Last chance?" asked Kristina.

"Yes, we're leaving here tonight after we drop you off."

"Oh."

Kristina was a little down hearted.

"I'm going to take you into space first though." Said Datch.

"OK." Said Kristina.

She was having so much fun with them she had forgotten that they were not from her world and would have to go home.

Datch pulled up a map of the city and found a bar that was just over a block away.

"That one looks good." he said.

"Yes, sounds like a plan." Said Carina.

They put the high vis vests on and headed outside.

Datch walked across to the attendant.

"Thanks for that. We're off for a beer now and we'll be back in a bit." He said and gave him another ten dollars.

"No problem, I'll stop till you go. I'm making loads of cash standing here anyway."

The news crew were looking at them and Datch had an idea and turned to Carina and Kristina.

"Follow me and just nod, ok?"

"What we doing?" Asked Kristina.

"Having fun." Said Datch.

He strode across towards the news crew.

"Hi." He said walking up.

"Hi." Said the guy at the front.

"I'm just checking, do you have the correct permits to film on the street and also is your parking meter paid."

"Ah, oh, one moment, I'll get them."

The man was looking flustered and went running back to the truck. Datch walked over to the parking meter. He looked at it. It appeared to be doing something but he wasn't sure what.

"Good." He said and looked at the others.

They nodded.

The man came back with some papers in his hand and handed them to Datch. He looked at them and then handed them back.

"Ok, they seem to be in order but try not to take up too much of the sidewalk can you. We don't want any of these folks to get knocked on to the road, do we?"

"Yes, sir. Err, I mean no sir."

"Great. Have a nice day."

"You too."

"Ok, you two, let's go. Everything seems in order here."

Carina and Kristina nodded and followed Datch past the crowd and set off down the street towards the bar.

Across the road two men sat on a seat watching them go.

Datch got a hundred metres down the road and took off his high vis vest and put it in a bag. The others did the same before carrying on down the street.

One of the men turned to the other.

"Did you see that?"

"What, the city workers?"

"They are not city workers."

"They aren't?"

"What city workers do you know that would appear under a space craft from nowhere and then give the parking attendant money before walking down the street taking their high vis off as they go and just stuff them into a rucksack?"

"Err. None, if they didn't like it, they would have called people in."

"Yes, and the high vis is a badge of office to them. They wouldn't take it off until they clock out at the office."

"Oh, so they are not city workers?"

"No. Come on."

The two men got up and followed Datch and the girls down the road and around the corner.

There, at the end of the street was a bar. It was quite a large bar and had seating outside on a raised area that ran along in front of the windows. The three of them reached the doors to the bar and went inside.

"They are defiantly not city workers." Said one of the men.

"No, they don't drink on duty."

They decided to wait for a few moments near the doors before following them inside.

The bar had a number of booths near the windows and around the edge the room. In the centre were a number of tall tables with bar stools and then at the back was the bar with two big tv screens, one on either side showing the sports channel which was currently showing a football game.

Datch headed over to the bar.

"Can I help you?" said the barman.

"Yes, we're after some food and a few drinks."

"Sure, if I can take your drinks order first?"

"Yes, can we have two beers and," He looked at Kristina and she nodded.

"Make that, three beers please."

"OK, if you would like to take a seat in one of the booths over there. You can take your pick, they are all free and I'll be over in a minute to sort out your food order."

They went over, sat down near the window and picked up the menus.

The door opened and two men came in and walked across to the bar. They sat down on two of the bar stools at the end of the bar so they got a good look at Datch.

The barman brought the beers over and placed them on the table.

"There you go. What can I get you food wise?"

"Can we have two steaks medium rare and one fish salad please."

"Sure, if you need anything just put your hand up and I'll come over."

"Ok thanks." said Datch.

The barman went back over to the bar and served the two men that had just come in.

Kristina looked at Datch.

"You're really going tonight?"

"Yes, we need to go back to our part of the galaxy. We've stopped longer than we meant to."

"I have really enjoyed the last two days. They have been a lot of fun in a funny sort of away. Are you sure you can't stop longer?"

"No, at some point, someone will see the Raven for what it is and then things will get messy."

"We have showed you too much as it is." Said Carina.

"Yes, anyway, let's just make the last few hours good ones, OK?" Added Datch

"All right."

"So, what is this game they are playing on the vi.. err, TV?"

"I think it's American football."

They sat watching it trying to work out what the teams were trying to do. The food came out and Datch did a scan to make sure it was ok before they tucked into it. The football game finished and so was the food. Datch was looking at the bar.

"What's up?" asked Carina.

'The two men over there. They are watching us.' Came Datch's voice inside her head.

'Are you sure?' she thought back

'Yes, they were also sitting on a seat across the street from the Raven watching it.'

'Oh, what do we do?'

'Not sure, but I have my pistol in my pocket if they are trouble.'

'I hope we don't need it.'

'I'm going over to the bar to have a closer look at them. Maybe if they know they have been spotted they will leave.'

'Ok, I'll watch your back.' said Carina.

Datch got up and started to walk over to the bar.

"What's going on?" asked Kristina sensing something was up.

"The two men over there are watching us. Datch is just going to make them realise that we've spotted them."

"Is that a good idea?"

"I don't know. We have Timbo to sort things out at home."

One of the men watched Datch walk across the room.

Datch stopped at the bar and looked straight at the men before turning to look at the bottles at the back of the bar.

"Well, it looks like it's time to introduce ourselves. You stay here in case the others make a run for it." Said one of the men to the other.

The man who seemed to be in charge got up and walked towards Datch.

'Look out, one of them is coming towards you.' came Carina's voice in his head.

Datch turned to look at the man as he approached and put his hand on the pistol in his pocket.

"Can I help you sir?" Asked Datch as he walked up.

"Yes, hit accept."

A box appeared in Datch's mind.

"What?" said Datch slightly shocked.

"Hit Accept."

Datch did and the shield of the Inter Planetary Space Federation appeared in his mind with officer Taymour underneath it.

"Oh..." said Datch looking worried.

"I think we need a little chat with you and your friends."

"You do?" said Datch hoping the answer would be no.

"Yes."

'Datch, what's going on?'

'They are IPSF officers'

'Oh, crap!'

"Shall we go?" Asked the officer.

"Err, ok."

Datch turned and started to walk to the table with officer Taymour.

Kristina looked at Carina and noticed that her face had changed from concerned too very worried.

"Who are they?" She asked.

"Err, they are sort of police."

"What American police?"

"No, our police."

"Your police.?"

"Yes."

"Oh, what do we do?"

"Just let me an Datch do the talking. It's not illegal for us to be here as long as we don't change the planets evolutionary course."

"Ok."

Datch arrived at the table with officer Taymour.

"This is officer Taymour, from the IPSF."

"Hello mam."

"Are we in trouble?" asked Carina.

"Well that all depends on what you have been doing."

"Now, please can you send me your ID's."

"Don't you just scan them?"

The officer looked a little uncomfortable for a moment.

"Err, we don't have the equipment. So please just send it to me."

He looked at Datch and Datch sent him his. He then turned to Carina and she sent him hers and finally he turned to Kristina.

"Err, I don't have one."

He screwed up his face for a moment while he tried to find an implant connection and couldn't.

"Err… why not?"

"I'm human."

"You're speaking Bellatrixian."

"Yes, but I'm human."

He turned to Datch and Carina.

"Datch, if she is human how come she is speaking Bellatrixian?"

Datch looked at the officer. He was not acting like a normal officer; something didn't seem quite right. He decided to ask a few questions himself

"Officer, I have some friends in the IPSF including three planetary presidents and a number of fleet captains. Can I have your ID please."

"Why?" now the officer was looking a little worried.

"Because I want to validate it. If you're an officer you are duty bound to give me your ID to validate it if I ask and I'm asking."

'What are you doing?' Came a voice in his head.

'Just follow my lead.'

"There would be no point. You can't validate it."

"Humour me." said Datch starting to grin.

The officer was looking a little unsure.

"OK. sure, why not."

Datch got his vid com out and placed it on the table.

"That's a vid com."

"Yes, please send your ID to it."

The officer stared at the vid com and then back at Datch. This was not the way it was meant to work. They should be scared of him.

"Well? unless you do, we are getting up and walking out of here."

"I'm sure my partner over there wouldn't like that."

"He won't like the plasma pistol in my pocket either. Now ID!"

Datch was starting to enjoy this, he could see the man was worried and starting to sweat.

"Ok."

A box appeared on the vid com. Datch hit select and an IPFS ID number appeared. Datch pressed a couple of keys and the vid com said 'please wait'

A moment later the officer's phone rang.

"I think you should answer that." Said Datch.

The officer took his phone out and answered it.

"Yes?"

"We're with them."

"What now?"

"OK. thanks."

Datch's vid com beeped. He looked at it and then turned to the officer.

"Oh, well, well what do we have here. Officer Taymour, rank science officer, currently assigned to studying the species of Sol three."

"What, how are you accessing that. You need an interspace link."

"We have an encrypted one in orbit and one further out in the system linking to the node at Sirius. So?"

"Err. Yes, we're here to study the humans."

Datch looked back at the vid com and continued,

"Duties included, studies of flora, fauna and to assess the humans threat level. Length of assignment seventy years. No access to tech above level three."

Datch looked at him.

"You're a science officer!"

The officer now looked like he had just been caught like a rabbit in the headlights.

"Err, Yes and?"

"You are not an enforcement officer and I take it you friend over there isn't either but just your assistant?"

"Well, yes but you still shouldn't be here. It might affect the planets evolution."

Datch sat back in his chair and looked at the officer. The officer was starting to wish he was at home watching the football game that was on the TV.

"Well, I'll still have to send a report about this." He said trying to assert himself."

"Hmm…" Said Datch thoughtfully.

"I take it, you're not meant to have any tech as you are using a human phone?"

"Yes, we're only allowed earth tech."

Datch's grin got bigger.

"So, how did you detect the signals from my vid com when I used it to connect to the ships coms?"

"Err, we just did."

"You built an interlink detector, didn't you?"

"We may have, what's wrong with that?"

"Well, it strikes me that you broke your own rules. That tech is at least a thousand years away by human technology levels, maybe more."

"Err… so?"

"So, I wonder what my friends will say when I tell them what you have been busy doing."

"OK, so we're fed up with this planet and wanted to try to connect to the galactic networks."

"Surely you have coms?"

"Well, they are using earth tech and we can only send reports using it. It transmits to an orbiting probe that relays them."

"I think you need to get your assistant to come over and tell your friend on the other end of the phone to turn off the scanner."

"Why?"

"Let's put it this way, we might get moaned at for coming to earth but you're likely to be stuck on this planet a lot longer without any chance of phoning home when they find out you have built a scanner."

The officer looked at him and had a thoughtful look on his face.

"Yes, but I haven't taught a human to speak Bellatrixian."

"True, so what do we do?"

The officer turned and beckoned to his assistant who came walking across the room to them.

"Hello." Said Datch grinning at him.

"Err, what's going on?"

"We're having a discussion." Said Taymour.

"What about the phone?" said Datch.

"Oh, yes."

He fetched out his phone and called the man back at their base.

"Hello."

"Yes, all is well. Err, please can you turn the scanner off."

"Yes, I know. Now turn it off."

"I don't care. Turn it OFF!"

"Thank you. I'll explain later."

He hung up.

"There, done."

"Good, now who is this and please drop the officer bit."

"This is Hopper."

"Hello Hopper. I am Datch, this is my wife Carina and our friend Kristina."

They all smiled at him. This was not the way he thought things were meant to be going.

"Err, Hello."

"So, Taymour what do we do?"

"Hmm. Well, I suppose we can forget about your visit if you can remove the matrix from the human's brain."

"Ah, we can't. It was a onetime thing the computer said."

"What?"

"Yes, we did it after we saved Kristina's life." Said Carina.

"You mean she should be dead as well?"

"Well, some men shot her and left her for dead in the jungle and we didn't want the animals to eat her."

Taymour looked at Datch and then Carina.

"The Amazon Jungle?"

"Err, yes."

"You didn't fire your weapon systems by any chance?"

Datch's grin decreased a bit.

"We may have." He said.

"OK, why don't you tell us what you have done. We picked up plasma weapons fire on our monitoring satellite which we have to keep an eye on the human weapon systems."

Datch looked at him thoughtfully for a moment. He was going to have to say something because of Kristina.

"Ok, we saved her and then got rid of the drug lord and his men so the tribe they were using as slaves, raping and killing could live without fear anymore."

"When you say 'got rid of' you mean killed."

"It was self-defence. We asked them nicely to go and they started shooting at us." Said Carina.

"Yes." Said Kristina trying to help defend their actions.

"Did any survive?"

"Only the drug lord and he was dragged off into the jungle by the remaining tribe members."

"That would be a no then."

Datch looked at him trying to gauge what he was thinking before continuing.

"That was it Taymour. Then we went to Roswell and had a steak before coming here."

"Why Roswell?"

"We needed some cash for the ice cream."

Hopper turned to Taymour.

"I told you we should have gone for an ice cream first."

Taymour stared at him and then turned back to Datch.

"OK, I take it you just got the ATM to give you the cash."

"Yes. I put it into maintenance mode and told it to test the vending system."

"OK. I can understand doing that. They are all insured anyway."

"So, you have things you would like to stay hidden and so do we."

He turned to Kristina,

"So, Kristina, tell me about your family?"

She looked at Datch. He nodded.

"My dad died a few years ago in the city and my mum and sister were killed by the drug lord's men."

"Don't you have anyone else?"

"No. not that I know of."

"Hmm…" He said.

Taymour sat back in his chair, thinking for a few moments before coming to a decision.

"OK, you took out the drug lord and his men, no loose ends there as the tribe probably think you're gods or something and the rest of your trip has been covert. The only issue I can see is Kristina."

"We're going to drop her back in the jungle." Said Datch.

"Yes, but she still has the matrix in her head not to mention that you've done things to her surgically."

"You did?" said Kristina looking worried.

"He means we gave you the nanobots that fixed your body up."

"Oh."

He looked straight at Datch.

"You'll have to take her with you."

"What?"

"You don't have a choice, it's either that or something will have to happen to her because if she comes into contact with any of the other IPSF officers here she'll start talking in Bellatrixian automatically and give us away. Oh, and before you ask there are nearly four hundred of us here at the moment."

"Four hundred?"

"Yes, we're doing an in-depth study on all their cultures."

"Err, don't I get a say?" asked Kristina.

They both turned to look at her.

"You are talking about my life aren't you."

"OK then, what do you think?" Asked Taymour.

She thought for a moment before answering.

"Ok, I've lost everyone I have ever known. The only people who know I'm alive are you and a hand full of people living in the jungle, who most likely now think I've been taken by the gods. So, if I can have the choice I'll go for space."

"You do know you will never be able to come back, don't you?" Said Taymour.

"Never?" Asked Kristina.

"Never!"

"Well, I still want to go to space."

Taymour turned back to Datch and Carina.

"Well, you two caused this so what's it going to be?"

Datch and Carina looked thoughtful for a moment.

'I say we take her' Came a voice in Datch's head.

'Yes, but what do we do with her?'

'A female backing singer would be nice.'

'OK, let's just hope she can sing.'

"OK, if we take her, you will forget we were ever here?" asked Datch.

"Will you give us access to the relay?" asked Taymour.

"OK, but it only has about ten years of power before it's supply will be depleted."

"That will be fine."

Datch turn back to Kristina.

"Kristina are you sure about this?"

"Yes." She said.

"OK. Do we have a deal Taymour?"

"Yes."

"Good. Let's have a drink to seal the deal." Said Datch and put his hand up to the barman.

They got a round of drinks and relaxed. Taymour and Hopper asked about the rest of the galaxy and if anything interesting had happened recently. Datch said to look out for The Pack in the news feeds but wouldn't say anything more. He then told them that when they got back to the ship, he would give them a portable interlink transceiver that could allow their implants to access the interlink relays and they could check the news for themselves.

The afternoon changed to early evening and it started to get dark outside. They paid the bill before leaving the bar to head back to the Raven.

They headed up the street and turned the corner towards the parking lot chatting as they went.

"So, I take it you're leaving now?" said Taymour in a tone of you better be.

"Yes, no point hanging around."

"Oh, make sure you get her an implant fitted."

"How can we do that?"

"You said you know people."

"Yes."

"So, pull a few strings."

"Hmm… Well, I'm sure I can ask a favour of someone."

As they arrived at the parking lot Datch, Carina and Kristina put on their High Vis vests. Datch turned to Taymour.

"OK, you wait next to the attendant's booth and we'll head inside, I'll bring the transceiver out and then I suggest you head over the road before we take off. That way you won't be seen."

"Ok. That sounds good to me."

Datch said hello to the attendant before heading over to the ship with the girls and disappeared inside.

A couple of minutes later Datch came back out with a bag and the vests. He walked over to Taymour and handed the bag to him.

"It's all set up, you just have to press the button on the top and pair it to your implants."

"OK. Have a safe trip home and try not to come back here again."

"We only came for ice cream."

"Ice cream?"

"Yes. Ice cream." Datch smiled at him. "Anyway, it will take a couple of minutes for me to do the pre-flight checks. I would say enjoy Earth but by the sounds of it, you're not. I've put the rest of the Earth money in the bag as well, I think there is about five or six thousand dollars left. It should get you a few beers."

"Thanks."

"OK. Well, if you're ever in Yuland city come to the Barbers inn and ask for me."

"We will."

Datch left them and walked over to the attendant.

"We'll be leaving in a couple of minutes so if you can make sure everyone keeps back. Thank you for all your help and have a great evening."

"You're welcome, sir. I hope the movie sells well."

"Thank you." Datch said and grinned.

He headed over to the Raven and disappeared inside.

Space

Carina was in the cockpit with Kristina as Datch came up the stairs. He walked over and sat down in the pilot's seat.

"OK, are you sure about this Kristina? last chance to get dropped off in the jungle." he said picking up his headset.

"Yes, I have nothing left on Earth and I don't want to spend my life living in the jungle. You only live once." She said.

Datch started to go through his pre-flight checks.

"Well, that's not true for you anymore." Said Carina.

"What do you mean?"

"Well, we didn't say anything before but the implant is not just for ID's. It is as a source of knowledge and information as well as recording images and vids. Also, we get four more bodies and the implant allows our brains to be transferred from one body to the other."

"Oh. So, you live for what, four to five hundred years?"

"Well, in Earth years it's about one thousand two hundred years per body or five hundred Bellatrixian years."

"So, you are going to live for seven thousand years?"

"Yes, and now you are going too as well."

"Me?"

"Yes, we'll sort out getting your implant fitted when we get home and you can live with us until you find your own path in life."

"Sorry to break into the conversation but we're ready to go. Everyone ready?"

"As ready as I can be." said Kristina.

"Let's go." Said Carina.

Datch brought the thruster online and outside the ship the down force blew the signs and barriers across the parking lot. The news crew turned to look at it and got their camera rolling. Across the road the two officers sat on the seat and sighed.

"I wish I was going with them." Said Hopper.

"Well, at least we can access the news networks now." said Taymour.

Datch increased power and the Raven lifted up into the evening air. He checked the proximity sensors, there was nothing in the local area. He pointed the nose up and pulled back on the main engines power control. The Raven shot into the sky accelerating as it went. The people below watched as the ship disappeared into the darkening sky.

The news reporter walked over to the parking lot attendant.

"I thought you said that was a helicopter?" Asked the reporter.

"Well, that's what they told me." Said the attendant.

The down force from the launch had blown papers and dust into the air. The seat across the road was now empty.

Datch brought the engines up to full power and the Raven reached orbital speed. Datch turned off the scattering field.

"Oh wow. Look at the Earth."

Outside the sun was lighting up one side of the atmosphere causing it to look like a diamond ring with light shining through it.

The Raven flew past the international space station more for fun than anything else and caused NASA to receive the message 'What the fuck was that!' and their response was 'ISS. You didn't see anything and neither did we.'

"Oh my god. We're in Space." Said Kristina watching it go past.

"Yes." Said Datch turning the Raven towards the moon.

Kristina looked at it in amazement. Its craters and features were now in sharp contrast and each valley and peak could be seen with shadows highlighting their topologies. There was none of Earth atmosphere to defuse the view and moon's surface was brightly lit by the sun.

Datch turned the ship again, this time the Earth was a dark sphere sitting in the stars. The light from the cities was creating a spider's web of light across the black disc that was the night side of Earth.

"Ok, Kristina. Time to go." Said Datch.

"Computer, Set a course for Luyten seven, interspace sixteen. Thirty-minute alarm please."

"Course laid in. Journey time will be two hours." replied the computer.

"Say good bye to Earth. You are about to travel faster than any human has gone before." Said Carina.

Kristina was looking outside. She watched as the ship turned away from earth and towards the stars.

'Well, this is it.' Kristina thought to herself. She was putting the rest of her life in the hands of two aliens that she had known for less than a week. Yet, here she was heading into the unknown with them. She felt a little apprehensive and nervous but at the same time excited about what lay ahead of her.

"Engage!" said Datch.

Kristina felt her stomach do a summersault and the stars outside winked out and started to flicker.

"Wow, what was that?" asked Kristina.

"Interspace sixteen." said Datch getting up.

"Err, don't you need to drive?"

"No. the computer's got it. Come on I need to book a villa on Luyten and we need to give you a crash course on the universe."

"Don't we need to go past Jupiter or Neptune?"

"They are already behind us. We are traveling at 6.8 light years per hour. The planet we are going to is 12.8 light years from Earth."

"So, we're in deep space?"

"Yes, and I'm going to the rec room for a drink. Also, I think you're going to need one."

"Why?"

"Well, we need to tell you what we do and who we are."

"I thought you already did that?"

"We sort of didn't say too much as you were a human and we didn't want to give too much away about our life. If you can understand that?"

Kristina thought about this for a moment.

"So, you lied to me."

"Oh no, everything we told you is true, we just missed bits out."

"Like what?"

They got to the rec room.

"OK. Maybe it's easier to start from the beginning." Said Datch getting some beers.

"Yes." agreed Carina.

He handed Kristina a beer.

"We are part or a rock band called The Pack. We are very well known in this part of the galaxy and we like to party."

"A rock band?"

"Yes," said Carina.

"Computer, please display information about The Pack." Said Datch.

The vid screen displayed a vid of The Pack on stage and down the side of the screen it listed the members and also listed facts such as they were the spiritual leaders of Welly four and savours of Arcaneus along with saving the president of Bellatrix five.

Kristina looked at it and then at Datch and Carina before looking back at the screen.

"So, why Earth?"

"Ice cream." Said Datch.

"Ice cream?"

"I like ice cream." Said Datch.

"Can you sing by the way?"

"Err, I don't know. I never really tried."

"Hmm. We need to get everyone together when we get back."

"Yes."

"Why?"

"Well, we were thinking of asking you to do backing vocals. But we'll sort that out later."

"Me? oh."

"Well, moving on." Said Carina.

"I just need to book a villa at the resort, so if you want to go through things Carina."

'Thanks!' Came Carina's voice in his head.

Datch sat down with his vid com.

"OK. Kristina, I had better start with your new home, Bellatrix."

Carina went on to explain about Bellatrix and how you were expected to behave. She was just talking about their schooling when Datch looked up from his vid.

"Ok, we're booked in. I have just had a thought though we're going to have to give you some more nanobots. The gravity on Bellatrix is about one and a half times that of Earth so we're going to have to build your mussels up a bit or you're going to struggle to get around."

"Will they hurt?" she asked.

"No, you swallow them like a pill and then they disperse into your blood stream. These ones will also stay in your body and keep it in tip top condition slowing your ageing process as well."

"So, I'll stop growing old?"

"Well, not stop. It will just take a very long time, as we said, our bodies last for five hundred Bellatrixian years."

"Oh, when do I get the pill then?"

"Computer, can you replicate standard repair and maintenance nanobots?"

"Yes, the replicator is able to produce them."

"OK Computer. Use the data from the medical scanner to program the nanobots and give them a home planet of Bellatrix five."

"A standard pack of Nanobots will be ready in five minutes please do not use any replicators until the task is complete as power is limited due to interspace drive systems."

"Thanks computer."

"Does the computer have a name?"

"Err, no."

"Why?"

"Well, we never thought about giving it one."

"Computer sounds boring. Can we give it a name?"

"Well, I suppose we can. Would Raven be less boring?"

"Yes. That sounds much better."

"OK. Computer. Please can you respond to the name Raven as well as the name Computer."

"Would you like to add personality as well?" asked the computer.

"No. We just want to use a name, that's all."

"I will now respond to both Raven and Computer."

"Thanks Raven."

Datch and Carina carried on by explaining about their lives and were just starting to talk about Welly four when Raven announced that the nanobots were ready. Datch got up and went over to the replicator. A small pack of five green pills was sitting on the replicator's tray. Datch picked them up and took them to Kristina.

"Here, these are your nanobots."

"Do I take all of them, I thought they would be smaller."

"Yes, you take all five. Each pill contains ten thousand nanobots."

"Wow, I'll have fifty thousand little machines running around in my body?"

She was looking a bit apprehensive.

"We are given them when we are two years old that's around five in earth years. You won't know you have them." said Carina.

"Yes, and they protect you from viruses and bacterial infections." added Datch.

She took a pill from the pack and looked at Datch and Carina. They nodded.

She put the pill in her mouth and took a drink of her beer. The pill didn't taste of anything. She swallowed it and waited. Nothing happened so she took a second one and then a third. Soon she had swallowed all five. She looked at Datch.

"Are they meant to be doing something?"

Datch smiled.

"They are, you just don't know it. You're probably going to get a hunger for steak, various meats and anything with a lot of protein or calcium in. They need to build your body structure up before you get to Bellatrix. Still, we're going to be spending a week at Luyten."

"Luyten?"

"Yes, Luyten seven. There is a very nice beach resort there with a lot of luxury villas and posh shops. I think we need time to get you up to speed with the rest of the universe and also over the culture shock before we take you home."

"This is going to be amazing." She said.

"Yes, it will."

They carried on telling the story of Welly four and then the ships alarm sounded.

"Looks like were nearly there."

Datch got up and headed to the cockpit followed by the girls. Kristina was eager to see another world and stood looking out of the cockpit window.

The view out of the front of the Raven was a little less than impressive as there were just stars flickering away. Datch sat down and put his head set on. Carina followed suit and sat in the co-pilot's seat.

"I can't see anything." Said Kristina peering out the front.

"We're still twenty minutes out." Said Datch.

Kristina sat down for the wait. They sat looking at the stars for another ten minute and then Kristina noticed that the one in the centre was getting brighter.

"Look!" She said.

"Yes, that's Luyten." Said Carina.

Datch pressed a virtual button to open a coms channel.

"Luyten Control, this is Starship Raven on approach to Luyten seven."

"Good morning, Raven, Traffic is light at the moment. Please lock on to beacon 334 for orbital approach and transmit your ID's and manifest."

Datch pressed some virtual buttons.

"Luyten Control, please be advised that we also have one alien with us who does not currently have an ID. We are currently in the process of sorting one out for her. She will be staying with us at all times."

"Raven, please state her point of origin."

Datch paused for a moment.

"Her point of origin is Sol three and the IPSF officers based there have given her clearance to be with us."

"Sol three has not made contact yet."

"Yes, we were checking out the flora and fauna when we were in contact with the IPSF officers. They asked us to bring her with us. They are processing her ID and she will be receiving her implant on Bellatrix five in a week's time."

"Please can you do a genetic scan and transmit please."

"Raven, please scan Kristina and send the genetic scan to Luyten control."

There was a short pause.

"Scan complete and data sent." Said the computer.

"Luyten control. Data has been sent."

"Thank you, Raven. Can you please confirm that she will be with you the whole time?"

"Yes, we take full responsibility for her while planet side."

"Please wait while I process the data and get clearance to issue the visa."

The bright star was now starting to get bigger.

"Raven, Visa has been approved with the condition she remains with you at all times. Visa ID is LYT1726-364-SOL3-017. I'll send a digital copy that should be attached to her for scanning if required."

"Thank you Luyten control, requesting beacon for Tarasands resort complex."

"Raven change to beacon TRS9321 on orbital interface."

"Thanks for your help, Luyten control. Raven out."

The star in the centre started to move to the side and a new bright disc appeared in the centre.

"Interspace will disengage in one minute." Said the Raven

Datch placed his hands on the controls. The disc was now getting very big.

Then the interspace drive disengaged and light flooded into the cockpit.

"WOW!" Said Kristina as Luyten seven appeared filling the whole of the view.

"Luyten control, this is the Raven. We are commencing planet fall. Locked onto resorts beacon."

"OK Raven. Enjoy your stay. Please contact Tarasands for final approach."

Datch turned the Raven in space and put her on the beacon's heading. The Raven descended dropping through the atmosphere. Plasma was cascading across the shields as the Raven dived down towards the planet's surface.

"Are we on fire?" asked Kristina looking worried.

"No, it's normal. It's just the planet's atmosphere hitting the Raven's shield."

Datch slowed the ship and the plasma vanished. Then they dropped through the high cloud and down into a clear blue sky.

"Oh my god. This is incredible. It's an alien world full of aliens." Said Kristina.

"Yes, but just remember, this is their world and you are the alien here. The galaxy is full of aliens but they are only aliens when they are not on their home worlds." said Carina.

"Tarasands control. This is the Raven on approach using beacon TRS9321. Requesting landing instructions."

"Good morning, Raven. Please land on pad seventeen.

"Tarasands control. Thank you. On final."

The Raven was now flying five hundred metres above the sea and in the distance was an island. As they approached, they could see pink sandy beaches with palm trees swaying in the breeze. In amongst the trees were a number of pools and restaurants. Then the landing area came into view. There were a few more ships sitting on their pads and to Kristina they all looked amazing. Datch brought the Raven in slowly and manoeuvred over pad seventeen before touching down with the slightest of bumps. Datch shut down the engines.

"Tarasands control. Raven has landed."

"Enjoy your stay, Raven. Control out."

Datch got up.

"Raven. Please create a visa module using the visa data sent from Luyten control. Make it suitable for attaching to Kristina allowing her to swim and shower without it becoming detached."

"The replicator in the recreational room has produced an adhesive pad containing all the information and it will respond to all types of scanners."

"Thanks Raven."

They headed to the rec room and there in the replicator was a small sticker that looked like a very tiny band aid.

"Carina, can you attach the visa please? While you do it, I'll go get our bags." said Datch

"Sure, no problem."

Datch headed off to their room. While Carina picked up the small pad. It was the same colour as Kristina's skin and was a couple of millimetres across.

"You'll need to have it on your neck as most of the scanners are aimed at the head. Here let me put it on for you."

"Err, how do I get it off when we leave?"

Carina stopped for a moment and asked her implant.

"We apply some solvent and the glue will soften letting it drop off."

"What was that look for?"

"What look?"

"You seemed to be staring into space for a moment."

"Oh that, you need to get use to that look. It happens when we access our implants. I was asking it how to get the visa off your neck."

"You mean you can just ask it things and it answers you?"

"Yes, that was what I meant when I said we didn't have school like you. Anything we want to know we can find out about as long as we have a connection. We couldn't use them much on Earth because the connection was so slow. Earth of course does not have access to the galactic network."

"Will I be able to do that when I get mine?"

"Yes. But don't worry about that now, we'll help you to get used to it when you have it implanted. Now, let me put this one you neck."

Kristina lifted up her hair and let Carina place the little device behind her ear.

"There, how does it feel?"

"I can't really tell it's there."

"Great."

"Are we ready folks?" said Datch walking in with two bags, one over his shoulder and the other in his hand.

"I don't have anything else to wear." Said Kristina.

"Hmm, good point. We'll have to take you shopping." Said Carina.

"Ok, I'll let you do that." Said Datch looking at Carina.

"Sure. I could do with a bit of retail therapy."

He then had a thought.

"Kristina, don't be shocked if you see any none human looking aliens, there may be some here. It's something you need to get used to. Please don't stare at them or you might offend them."

"OK. I'll try not to."

"Cool, let's go."

They headed to the cargo bay and the way out.

At the bottom of the ramp two men were standing waiting for them.

"Welcome to Tarasands resort. Do you require anything for your ship?"

"Yes. Please could you refuel it for me."

"Certainly Sir. Do you need anything else?"

"Yes, are there any good clothing shops nearby by any chance, our friend here is a bit short of clothes?"

"Yes sir, if you head to the back of the resort and down the road to the village there are one or two shops on the back streets that sell clothing items."

"Thank you, add a ten-credit tip for yourselves."

"Thank you, sir. You can find the main resort over there through the gate. Also, if you require anything please do not hesitate to ask a member of staff."

"Thanks."

They headed off to the main reception where they checked in. After signing in a porter came over to escort them to their villa. He had four arms which as he was a porter came in very handy. Kristina looked at him and her jaw dropped.

"Is there a problem mam?" He asked.

"Sorry, no, she is new to travelling and you are the first Hexman she has seen." Said Carina.

"Yes, sorry, I didn't mean to stare." Added Kristina.

"No Problem mam. Very understandable if you haven't seen a Hexman before. If you would like to follow me to your villa."

They followed him out of the main doors and across the resort towards the villas. The porter was very friendly chatting away to Kristina and explaining about his world where everyone had four arms.

They arrived at the villa, it was surrounded by a hedge that provided privacy and it had its own splash pool and sauna along with a large sun terrace.

Inside it had four bedrooms all with ensuites, an automated kitchen just in case you wanted to eat in, a very large lounge with vid screen to match and an open plan dining room.

Kristina was looking in awe at the villa. She had never seen anything like this before.

Datch put the bags in one of the bedrooms and he turned to the girls.

"Carina, why don't you take Kristina shopping while I send an email to Widfab. I'm going to ask if he can sort out an implant and ID for Kristina."

"What about Coola?"

"He will ask to many questions. Widfab will just say ok dude."

"Ah, I see what you mean. Right, Kristina lets go shopping."

"But how can I pay for it?"

"We'll get them. We told you we would take care of you until you find your feet."

"I think we'll need to have a nap next to the pool when you get back as it's not even lunch time yet." Said Datch.

"Lunch? It was evening when we left."

"Yes, I suspect it will be about nine in the evening in LA."

"And its morning here?"

"Welcome to galactic travel." Said Datch.

"Come on, Lets go." Said Carina.

"Ok, see you later, I'll be next to one of the pools when you get back."

"OK."

With that the girls left and Datch fetched his vid com out of his pocket. This was not going to be easy. He sat down and started the email.

'Hi Widfab, we are having a great time on honeymoon and thanks for the fantastic gift of the kabab machine. We have been having so much fun that I need a small favour…'

He went on to explain that they had saved Kristina but, in the process, ended up with her coming with them. He explained about the IPSF and asked if he wouldn't mind keeping that part to himself and then finished with 'Party on Dude, Datch and Carina.'

He sat back and read it twice making a few adjustments in the process. He pressed the send button and sat there for a moment. He then sent Fred a message asking if they could all meet in the Barbers in eight days' time saying that he had a surprise for them.

Afterwards he put his trunks on and headed to the pool for a nap in the sun.

Carina and Kristina headed down a small lane that led to the village.

"Datch is really something isn't he?" Asked Kristina.

"Yes, life is always interesting around him."

"How long have you two been together?"

"Oh, about ten of your years. We fell in love at school. It was pretty much love at first sight."

"Cool."

"Let's go in here."

They went in looking at the clothes.

"I feel guilty about causing all this trouble." Said Kristina as they walked around the shop.

"We sort of have a soft spot for people in trouble. Getting involved sort of makes life less dull. Also, we like helping people. What do you think about this?" said Carina showing her a nice top.

"Yes, it looks nice."

Carina scanned it in.

"So, what made you help me?"

"We couldn't just leave you there to die. That's not us."

"Yes, but look at what's happened."

"This is nothing, Last time we ended up being chased across the stars by a battleship that was hell bent on destroying us. Now that was scary."

"Oh my god. How did you escape?"

"We had help from some very good friends and the battleship ended up being taken away for scrap."

"They must be very powerful friends."

"Not really, one is the captain of a galactic starship and is a bit like a second father to Datch. Datch saved a number of Dons crew along with his dad when he was five. Sorry twelve in Earth years. Do you like this?" said Carina point to a bikini.

"Wow. Err, can I have that one over there?"

"Yes, Sure. Anyway, we found out about it from the bikers when Datch took us to the Barbers inn for the first time. I was in awe at what he had done and I suppose I fell for him."

"By the sounds of it, you live a busy life."

"Yes, it's hard work with the band. The hero stuff is sort of a break for us. I know that must sound strange."

"No, I can sort of understand it. On Earth we have a saying, a change is as good as a rest."

Carina laughed.

"I'm going to remember that one."

They paid for the clothes and afterwards went into another shop this time it was much bigger and catered for alien wear.

Kristina stood looking at it trying to work out what it was.

"That is for a humanoid with three legs." Said Carina helpfully.

"Oh, I never thought about that."

"Yes, some aliens have more than two legs and some have more than the normal number of arms like the Hexman you saw earlier. The galaxy is full of different lifeforms and normally we all live side by side with each other."

"Don't you have wars?"

"Not really, the IPSF makes sure of that."

"They have that much power?"

"Yes. I'll tell you about Arcaneus later. We witnessed it first-hand. They don't mess about."

"So that was why you were worried back on Earth."

"Well, we thought we may get told off a bit. Earth is not off limits as such but we're not meant to make direct contact."

"So, with me being with you it meant you were in trouble?"

They found some more clothes that Kristina liked and this time put them in a basket that they had picked up on the way in.

"Well, I think we were more in trouble for parking the Raven in the middle of LA."

"Oh."

"But then the Datch effect happened."

"The Datch effect?"

"Yes, things just happen around him. He spotted that they were not following orders and then he had the upper hand. If they had complained about us, they would have been in a heap of trouble themselves."

"So, we won?"

"Sort of, Datch needs to sort out the implant bit and also his dad won't be happy."

"His dad?" Kristina hadn't thought about how their family would react.

"Yes, he's a retired commander of the IPSF, so he may be a bit annoyed with Datch."

"Oh."

"Don't worry, you won't see it. Anyway, what do you think of this?"

The conversation turned back to clothes. Then, after filling the basket they had to buy a bag to carry all the clothes in. They went in another shop and got a few more before they headed back to the resort.

They put the clothes in Kristina's room at the villa and changed into their bikinis before heading into the main complex to find Datch.

They found him sleeping on a sunbed under a palm tree.

"Datch!"

He looked up. Standing in front of him were the two girls looking stunning. He looked at them and closed his eyes again.

"Datch!"

"Err, Hi." he said trying to wake himself up.

"You, ok?"

"Yes, I just fell asleep, sorry."

"Did you get the implant sorted?"

"I sent a message to Widfab but I bet it will take a while for him to get it."

The girls sat down.

"Can I get something to eat?"

"Sure, we could all do with a snack."

"I'm starving." Said Kristina.

Carina put up her arm and a waiter came over.

"May I help you, mam?"

"Yes, we would like a Traxsent starburst, a beer and,"

She looked at Kristina.

"Do you want a starburst too?"

"I don't know what it is but why not?"

"Two starbursts please. Also, some fries, and a small bucket of hacks wings. What do you want to eat Kristina?"

"I'm very hungry, do you do beef burgers?"

"She means Jaxx burgers?"

"Yes mam, small or large?"

"Can I have two large ones and a large fries please?"

"Certainly mam."

"Give yourself a two credits tip as well." added Carina.

"Thank you, mam." Said the waiter and headed off to fetch the drinks.

Datch was starting to wake up a bit more now.

"You two look great." He said trying to make up for the being asleep bit.

"Thanks." They said.

He sat up on his sunbed.

"Did you get Kristina some clothing?"

"Yes, we found a few outfits, so she's good for now."

"I can't thank you enough for all this."

"You're welcome. When we get back home, I'm going to take Kristina to the mall and we'll get her a full wardrobe."

"Sounds good."

Kristina was looking around at the pool area. Carina sat on the sunbed next to Datch. They had just sat down when Datch's vid com pinged. He picked it up and looked at it.

"Wow, that was fast!"

"What?"

"Widfab, he must still be on Bellatrix. It would have taken a couple of days otherwise."

"What's he say?"

"He won't be there when we get back but he's having an implant sent to the embassy and for us to take Kristina there as soon as we get back. He has told immigration that we are bringing someone with us and has given us a visa number which will last until she gets the implant."

"Oh. anything else?"

"He's told the embassy staff not to ask any questions and not to bow too much as we don't like it."

"Cool."

"He also says, it sounds like we're having fun and he hopes we enjoy the kabab machine he gave us."

"Hmm, I'm not sure where we're going to put it?"

"I'll get dad to help me extend the patio area when we get back. We can put it at the end near the barbeque."

"Yes, and we can put the new patio set under the veranda next to it."

Just then the waiter came back followed by a second one. he passed the girls their drinks and then handed Datch his beer after which he put a cloth over the small table and relieved the second waiter of the food.

"Please, enjoy." He said.

They turned and headed off back towards the bar.

"Wow, that's a lot of food." Said Datch.

"Most of it is Kristina's." Said Carina.

"Are you sure you can manage that?" Asked Datch

"I think so, I'm feeling very hungry." Said Kristina looking at the food.

They set about the food. Well, Kristina did. She looked like she was on a mission. The burgers didn't last long and then she demolished the fries. Datch and Carina watched in amazement as she put it all away.

She turned to them.

"Are we having dessert?"

"You can if you like, I'm saving myself till later." said Carina.

"Me too."

"Oh, that's right it's only lunch time."

"I don't know why I'm so hungry."

"It's the nanobots building your body up. Give it a couple of days and you'll start feeling stronger." Said Datch.

"Cool. So, what are we doing now?"

"Having a nap." Said Carina.

"I don't feel tired, can I go for a walk?"

"Only around the complex, if you're found outside the complex without us, you'll get arrested and we'll get in a lot of trouble."

"OK. I'll make sure I stay inside it."

She got up and walked off.

Datch and Carina settled down on the sunbeds.

"Do you think she will be ok?" said Carina when she was out of earshot.

"What you mean wandering off?" Said Datch.

"No, when we get back home. She's going from living in a jungle to somewhere thousands of years more advanced. She could feel a bit out of her depth."

"Hmm, I see what you mean. I'm sure she'll be ok though. We'll be there for her until she adjusts to it all. The implant will help her anyway."

"I am a bit worried. She is our responsibility."

"It will be fine. Look at it as practice for when we have kids."

"Hmm. OK."

"Right, let's have a nap. She's got thousands of nanobot working like mad keeping her awake. Most of ours are dormant at the moment."

"OK."

They laid on their backs enjoying the warm sun on their skin and nodded off.

Kristina walked down to the beach. The sand was a pink colour due to the red sandstone that formed part of the island. The sea was a beautiful blue colour with a hint of turquoise in it. She found a spot under a tree and sat down.

It was the first time she had been alone since this all started. Here she was on an alien world sitting under a palm tree looking out at the sea. See looked up into the sky looking for Earth before realising that she wouldn't be able to see it. She felt alone for a moment, lost in her thoughts of home and a place she would never see again. Then she looked across the sea again just in time to see another ship on approach to the island. It flew straight in from the sea and seemed to be going so slow she thought it should drop out the sky. Her eyes followed it until it disappeared over the trees. She looked back out to sea. 'Well, I'm here now, no turning back and so far, it's been quite amazing' she thought trying to make herself feel better. She looked down at the beach.

"I bet Earth doesn't have pink sand." She said to herself and smiled.

Some of the leaves on the bushes and trees also had a pink tinge in them that gave the view a very alien look.

She got up and went for a walk along the beach. Group of small lizards came running out of the bushes heading straight towards her. She froze to the spot and was about to scream when they split into two groups and went around her heading to the water. She let out a sigh of relief and watched them enter the sea and swim out in a shoal or group. 'What do you call a group of lizards?' she thought. She carried on her walk along the beach cooling her feet off in the sea as the waves lapped gently on the shore.

It was late afternoon when she arrived back at the sunbeds. Datch was awake when she arrived but Carina was still sleeping.

"Did you have a nice walk?" he asked.

"Yes. It let me get my head straight a bit and it was quite something walking on an alien world for the first time."

"Yes, I remember my first-time off world. I went to a desolate hole called Asmove."

"Why?"

"My dad thought it would be fun which it was sort of, but planet itself was not good."

"What's not good?" Came a voice from the other sunbed.

"Err, Asmove."

"Oh, are you telling the story?" asked Carina.

"No, just talking planets."

"Well, I'm starting to feel a bit peckish now. Why don't we head back to the villa to get changed and then go to the restaurant for dinner?"

"Sounds good. I'm getting hungry again, must have been the walk."

"No, Nanobots." Said Datch and Carina together.

"Oh, them, I forgot about them." said Kristina looking at her stomach.

"Yes, we all do." said Carina.

Datch put his hand up and a waiter came over.

"Yes, sir?"

"Can we get a table for three in the restaurant?"

"Yes, sir. What time?"

Datch looked at the girls,

"In about an hour?" He said, the girls nodded.

"Certainly sir."

"I noticed there is karaoke on tonight, what time does it start?"

"That is in the main bar at around seventeen hundred, sir."

"Thank you."

"You're welcome, sir."

They got up and started to walk back to the villa.

"That's an odd time for karaoke." said Kristina.

"Sorry, I forget to tell you. We're on a twenty-hour clock here. Twenty hours and one hundred minutes each hour."

"What about the seconds?"

"One hundred per minute."

"Oh. So what time is seventeen hundred?"

"Err, on the twenty-four clock it's about eight thirty ish."

"I just remembered, we left earth in the evening."

"Yes, so to us it's about three in the morning." Added Carina.

"Wow, and I don't feel tried."

"Nanobots!"

"Oh."

"Don't worry, they will start to slow down tomorrow or the day after." Said Carina.

"They will have added a lot of extra muscle mass to your body by then and also a lot of bone." Added Datch.

"I feel stronger already."

"Hopefully, you will be ready for Bellatrix when we get there. Although you will be sleeping a bit, sort of making up for the next few days. Your body is in overdrive at the moment."

They arrived back at the villa and headed off to shower.

Datch sat on the sofa going through his emails and messages when the girls walked out of the bedroom. He looked up.

They both looked amazing, dressed in knee length skirts and light flowing tops. Datch put his vid com down.

"Wow, you both look great." He said.

"Thanks." They both said.

"Shall we go?"

He got up and put his arms through theirs and they headed across the resort to the restaurant for dinner.

Kristina had a very large helping of food including two starters, the largest Jaxx steak on the menu and followed it down with three bowls of chocolate ice cream. It was like pouring food into a bottomless hole. Food kept going in and she kept eating. After the food, they finished their drinks and headed over to the main bar.

"Ok, this is going to be a bit strange but just watch and listen. We're going to do a song called Star Lovers as we need to boost our telepathic link. We tried it earlier and it wasn't working."

They sat and watched as a few more people went up and did a few songs and then it was Datch and Carina's turn.

They ran to the stage and grabbed the mics.

"Hello, Tarasands." Said Datch.

The bar cheered for no reason they could think of but they did it anyway. Datch nodded to the karaoke operator and Star Lovers started to play. The two of them started to sing and then as they came together on stage their rings started to shine brightly and sparkles started to cascade down their bodies. Then, as the song continued, they started to glow green, a bright luminous green.

People started dancing and sparkles appeared around them. Kristina watched as Datch and Carina danced around each other trailing a green glow behind them as they moved. It was like watching magic happen in front of her eyes. Then, they came together for the kiss. The light surrounding them now became one column of light and a blast of green energy went across the room. The song came to an end and Datch and Carina left the stage to a huge round of applause.

Kristina looked at them and then realised that sparkles were coming off her head. She poked some and found that nothing happened, they just disappeared into her finger.

"What did you think?" said Carina sitting down.

Both her and Datch were glowing brightly.

"That was very, err, wow, incredible and different?"

The both laughed.

"I take it you liked it."

"Yes. Err, do these sparks set fire to things?"

"No, but you will feel good for a few days." Said Carina.

"Cool. Err, can I poke your aura?"

"Well, no one has ever asked that before." said Carina.

"Oh, sorry, I didn't mean it to come out like that."

Carina laughed.

"Go on then, have a poke."

Kristina put her finger near Carina's arm. The tip of her finger glowed for a moment but stopped as soon as she moved it away.

"Wow." she said, "If you did that on Earth someone would start a religion around you and the pope would want to see you."

"Who is this pope guy?"

Kristina looked at them for a moment trying to work out if they were joking. Then it dawned on her that they had no idea who he was.

"Oh, right. He's the head of the Catholic church on Earth."

"Is he a demigod?" Asked Datch.

"Err, I don't think so. why?"

"Oh, OK. It doesn't matter, I just wondered if he partied much."

"I don't think he would, not in his position. Anyway, he's getting quite old now."

"Maybe we could go and take him to a party and find out?"

"Kristina?" said Carina changing the subject before Datch got any ideas about going back to Earth and kidnaping this pope guy.

"Yes?"

"As you can read Bellatrixian now. How do you fancy doing a song with me later?" asked Carina.

"Err, I don't read Bellatrixian."

"You have been since you left Earth. Everything we have showed you has been in Bellatrixian."

"Oh, has it?"

"Yes."

Kristina started to think about what she had been reading and then realised that the symbols were totally different.

"I have, haven't I?"

"Yes. So, what about a song?"

"I don't know, I've never really done any singing before, let alone alien songs. I've only ever sang along to the radio sometimes."

"You will be fine and if we wait a bit, it won't matter how you sing as everyone will have had a few drinks and their implants will translate the Bellatrixian you're singing into their language anyway."

"I don't want to make a fool of myself."

"You'll be fine." Said Carina reassuringly.

"OK then, I'll do it. Will I glow like you?"

"Err, no, you'll just sparkle a lot." Said Datch.

He put his hand up and a waiter came over.

"Can we have another round of drinks please."

"Certainly sir, do you require anything else?"

"Can I have some nuts please?" Asked Kristina.

"We do a number of verities, Peezer's, Banyo, Pupper and Banban. Which would mam like?"

 Kristina looked at Carina,

"She'll have Peezer's dry roast please."

"A large bowl please?" Said Kristina smiling.

"Certainly, Is that everything?"

"Yes, thank you and give yourself a five-credit tip." said Datch.

"Thank you, sir."

The evening went on and Kristina continued to ask for food. It was like watching a machine devour everything that was put in front of it. Datch started to wonder if the Raven had made too many nanobots. They were certainly very busy that's for sure.

They were just on their third round of drinks when Carina's and Kristina's names were called.

"Come on." Said Carina getting up.

"I'm a bit nervous." Said Kristina standing up.

"Don't be, the writing on the screen will be in Bellatrixian, so the matrix in your brain will translate it for you. Just sing what you see on the screen in front of you."

"OK, I'll try."

They headed up to the stage and were given a round of applause. Datch started recording it with his implant.

The words to the song appeared on the screen and Supernova started to play. They started to sing and Kristina after a shaky start soon got into the swing of it. By the end of the song, she was singing the chorus without reading the screen. Datch was watching her very closely and was quite impressed by what he could see and hear.

The song finished to a huge round of applause and Carina and Kristina bowed to the audience before leaving the stage. They came back to the table and sat down. Datch stopped his implant and stored the file.

"So, what did you think?" asked Carina.

"You were very good." Said Datch.

"Thanks." Said Kristina.

Datch looked at Carina.

'She'll need a bit of fine tuning but she could certainly do backing vocals' said a voice in Carina's head.

'Yes, she can belt out the notes. Maybe we could do a girl's song?'

'That's not a bad idea. Maybe we could do a boy's song as well.'

'OK, but back to Kristina, as long as the others like her and she wants to do it. Are you happy to give her a go?'

'Yes, I think she will be fine.'

"You two are doing the telepathy thing again, aren't you?"

"Err, yes." said Datch looking surprised.

"I can tell when you do it because the expressions on your faces keep changing when you're looking at each other."

"Oh, sorry, it's a bit like talking behind your back."

"No, it's ok, I expect it was husband and wife stuff so it's cool."

"Yes, sort of, we were just making sure it was working."

"Can we go up again?"

"What to sing?"

"Sure, what about the three of us?" Added Datch.

"That's a good idea." Said Carina.

"Ok, Wild Wind." Said Datch.

"OK."

"Wild Wind?" Asked Kristina.

"Yes." said Datch and grinned.

It took another ten songs before they were called back on stage and then the three of them set the bar a light. By the end of the song Kristina was a water fall of green sparkles and most of the people in the bar had sparkles coming from their heads.

They went back to their table and had another round of drinks before heading back to the villa and to bed. Datch had done a calculation and they had been up for thirty-eight hours with only the afternoon naps to keep them going.

The rest of the week flew by. They went out to sea on a boat and did some scuba diving exploring a local reef. Another shopping trip into the village was also in order followed by a very nice meal at a fish restaurant. Half way through the week Kristina's food intake started to dropped back to normal. Datch took her on the Raven and did a quick scan to make sure everything was OK. The scanner showed that the nanobots had built her bones and muscle mass to levels that were good for Bellatrix.

They spent the last couple of days chilling by the pool and down on the beach. Finally, it was time to head home.

Bellatrix

Datch sat in the cockpit going through the pre-flight checks. He had just about finished when the girls came up the stairs.

Datch looked over his shoulder as they walked along the corridor and sat down.

"OK folks, Time to go home. Err, your new home to be, in Kristina's case."

Datch turned to the front and put his headset on.

"Tarasands control, this is the Raven ready for departure. Destination Bellatrix five."

"Good morning, Raven. Your cleared for take-off, lock on to beacon T234J19 and follow to orbit. You will be clear to navigate after leaving orbit. Traffic is currently light."

"Thanks, Tarasands, locking on to beacon."

Datch increased thrust to the manoeuvring thrusters and the Raven lifted off. He locked on to the beacon and accelerated into the sky. The sky slowly turned from light blue to black and the stars came out.

Kristina watch as Datch turned towards Bellatrix, a bright star moved to the centre of their view. That star was going to be her new home. She was filled with trepidation about her new world. Would it be an incredible place or a nightmare? Datch and Carina had talked to her at length about her new world during the last few days but, would it be all they said it was?

The stars winked out and started to flicker.

Datch got up.

"OK time for a bit of Solar Ball."

"Come on Kristina, we'll have you playing like a pro by the time we get home."

"OK, but it may take me a while to pick it up."

"We've got thirty-four hours until we get there."

"That's a long time."

"Yes, it's two hundred and fifty light years." Added Carina.

"Will I be able to see the sun from there?"

"You mean Sol. No, your star is too dim to be seen on Bellatrix with the naked eye. You would need a sensor array to get an image of it. Just remember though that any images you see are two hundred and fifty years old."

"Oh."

They arrived at the cargo bay and activated a game of Solar Ball. They started to teach Kristina how to play. They spent most of the day playing and then stopped up watching movies until the following morning as the time difference meant they would be arriving at lunch time. They slept until the early evening which was in fact morning in Yuland city. Yes, Intergalactic travel is very confusing.

Datch had set an alarm for nine thirty Yuland city time and they got up and headed to the rec room for coffee.

"This feels strange." Said Kristina.

"What?"

"Having breakfast at dinner time."

"Yes, but it's breakfast time. Its space, worlds orbit and rotate at different speeds. It's a bit like catching an aircraft from LA and landing on the other side of the world it could be morning when you arrive even though you left in the afternoon."

"I see what you mean. Is it a twenty-hour clock?"

"No, it's twenty-four-hour clock."

"Good, because that would be confusing."

"Raven, set the clocks to display Yuland city time please."

The clock changed and was showing ten thirty.

"Is that ten in the morning?" asked Kristina.

"Yes, we have just over an hour before we need to head to the cockpit."

They sat drinking their coffees.

"What do you think your dad will say about me?"

"He'll be ok, I'll just get moaned at a bit about going to Earth. I've sent him a message telling him about what happened and that you are with us. I also told him when we were arriving and that we have to go to the embassy soon after arrival for you to get your implant."

"What did he say?"

"I don't know. he's not answered yet."

"Knowing your dad, he'll wait till you get there and then drag you into the bar." said Carina.

"Yeh, I'll prompt it, I think. That way it will be over and done with." Said Datch.

"Will he say anything to me?" asked Kristina.

"No. He'll be fine with you, it's my ass he'll chew off."

"Oh, sorry."

"You don't have anything to be sorry for. We did this, not you. So, don't think it's your fault for even a moment. It will all be good, I promise."

"Yes, we both do." Added Carina.

"Anyway, Fred has come back to me and they are all going to the Barbers for mid-afternoon. So, if we can get there for three ish. If you're ok Kristina, we can have dinner there."

"I'm a bit nervous about meeting everyone to be honest."

"Don't be. They are all really cool." Said Carina.

Datch put the vid on and asked the computer to play the news channels for Yuland city. It took a few moments to download the mornings bulletins before it started to play them. There wasn't anything really interesting but Kristina was watching them intently. It was the first live images of her new home and gave her an insight into the world she was about to set foot upon. The news itself was pretty boring. There had been a new statue unveiled of the president near the new power plant, A new wing at the hospital had been opened with a research section and there was going to be a carnival in the city next month.

"How come there is no weather?" Asked Kristina.

"Oh, that. It happens between five and six in the morning. Then the rest of the day is sunny." Said Datch.

"Wow, so we never get wet?"

"Well, no, unless you go out at five in the morning. The weather is controlled most of the time but in the winter, we get tornados and large super storms which are allowed to do their thing. They tend to be too big to control and most of the buildings have shielding anyway."

"Shielding?"

"Yes, like the Ravens shields but around the buildings."

"What if they don't have them?"

"Well, normally they need a new building." Said Datch.

"Oh."

"We have a shield at the ranch so the rain doesn't even get in. You can sit outside and watch the rain pour down the sides of the shield. It's pretty cool to watch sitting next to the pool." Added Carina trying to lighten the mood.

Datch looked at the clock.

"Well, it looks like it's time to head to the cockpit." He said getting up.

They all headed to the cockpit and sat down. Outside the stars were flickering away and there was a large bright star in the centre of their view.

"How far away are we?"

"Oh, about a light year away. But I need to get locked on to a beacon as the space here is a lot busier than that around Luyten."

He put his headset on and pressed a couple of virtual buttons.

"Bellatrix control, This is the starship Raven inbound from Luyten heading for private landing area 647 outside of Yuland city. Requesting auto navigation."

"Good morning, Raven. Please lock on to beacon 2345Y71 for auto navigation. Be advised traffic is heavy."

"Bellatrix control - Locking on to beacon now."

Datch pressed a few buttons.

"Raven please transmit your ID's and manifest."

"Bellatrix control. We do not have cargo but have a passenger on visa BELYUL2394D7. She will be receiving her implant shortly after arrival at the Welly four embassy."

"Raven please stand by."

They waited and a moment later the comms burst back into life.

"Raven, visa is confirmed, please keep her with you until the implant is installed."

"Understood control."

"Auto navigation confirmed. Welcome home and enjoy the ride."

"Thanks Control, Raven out."

The bright star was getting very bright now and then it started to move up and another bright point of light took its place in the centre of the view.

"Interspace drive will disengage in two minutes." Said the computer.

They watched as the small point of light got bigger and bigger. Then the interspace drive disengaged and light flooded into the cockpit. Bellatrix sat in front of them shining brightly in the darkness of space. The Raven fell in behind another ship joining a line of ships heading for the surface.

"Wow! It's so beautiful! Oh my god, look at all the ships."

Kristina watched in awe as the Raven followed the ships downwards towards the planet. The shields lit up with plasma streams as they hit the atmosphere. Kristina could see the ship in front was surrounded by fire as it dived down into the atmosphere and then as fast as the fire appeared it vanished and they were in a sky with a greenish tint. Below them was a desert with rolling sand dunes.

"Raven, this is Yuland control. Beacon will disengage in thirty seconds."

"Thanks, Yuland control."

Datch put his hands on the controls, Below the desert got closer and closer. Datch watched the countdown in his heads-up display.

"Raven, you have control."

"Thanks, Yuland city."

Datch banked the Raven to the left away from the main stream of traffic. Kristina was getting very excited as well as nervous. In the distance was a city made of glass towers shining in the sun. Up ahead the desert turned from sand to scrubland and then a ranch came into sight with a large landing pad next to one of barns. A bright beacon started flashing on the pad. Datch slowed the ship down to fifty KPH and brought the landing thrusters online. The Raven slowed to a stop and Datch turned her so she was facing the city before dropping her gently down onto the landing pad.

"Yuland Control, Raven has landed."

"Thanks Raven. Have a good day. Yuland Control out."

Datch shut down the engines and turned to Kristina.

"Welcome to Bellatrix." He said.

"Thank you." She said.

"Ok, let's go find mum and dad." He said getting up.

They headed to the cargo bay and opened the cargo bay before trotting down the ramp. Tansya came walking over from the house and met them halfway across.

"Hello folks." She said and smiled.

Datch walked up and gave her a hug.

"Hi mum."

Then it was Carina's turn.

"Mum, we would like you to meet Kristina. Kristina this is my mum Tansya." Said Datch.

"Pleased to meet you." Said Kristina.

"Yes, nice to meet you too. Welcome to Bellatrix." Said Tansya. She turned to Datch as they started to walk towards the house.

"So, it sounds like you have had an exciting honeymoon?"

"Yes, you could say that. Err, is Dad, ok?"

"Yes, he's ok. Slightly annoyed but he's calmed down now. Most people go on holiday and bring back souvenirs not an entire alien."

"It just sort of happened."

"Oh well, never mind but I think your dad will moan at you later, he's nipped into the city to get something from the DIY store. Come on, I bet you all could do with a drink and something to eat?"

"Yes, but we have to get Kristina to the Welly four embassy this afternoon for her implant and we're meeting the gang in the Barbers afterwards."

They walked over to the pool and sat down. Carina went in with Tansya to help fetch the drinks and some Jeader rolls.

"This is amazing. Do you live here?" she said looking at the ranch house.

"No, our home is over there." Datch said pointing at the barn conversion.

"Oh, that's cool. Nice and close to your mum and dad then?"

"Yes, and very handy for the pool."

She sat looking around and then across to the city in the distance

"I know I asked you before but are you sure the implant doesn't hurt?"

"No, it doesn't hurt, you'll be fine and afterwards you will also see the universe in a totally different light."

"Oh."

She thought for a moment.

"Will it change me?" She asked.

"No, you will still be you, but you won't need to ask about things as much."

"What do you mean?"

"Well, if you want to know what something is at the moment you have to ask us. When you have your implant, you can just ask it and the answer pops straight into you mind. It makes life a lot easier in restaurants that's for sure."

"I'm still nervous though."

"Me and Carina will be standing right next to you, so don't worry."

"Ok." she said relaxing a bit.

"I know you showed me the pictures of Bellatrix. But the sky, it looks so different." She said.

"Yes, I know what you mean, we felt the same when we went to a world with a blue sky, but you get used to it. It's the argon gas that gives it a green tint but don't worry it's safe to breathe."

Just then, Carina came back out with Tansya carrying some cups of coffee and plate of Jeader rolls.

"So, Kristina, you're from Earth?" Said Tansya sitting down.

"Yes, Brazil."

"Is that hot or cold?"

"Err, hot. It's a bit warmer than here anyway."

"Well, this is winter so it will warm up in the summer. What did you do on Earth?"

"I lived with my dad in the city until he died unexpectedly and then I moved to live with my mum and sister in the jungle until they were killed." She started to look down.

"You're safe with us now." Said Carina stepping in.

"Sorry, I didn't mean to upset you." Said Tansya.

"It's OK, everything has just happened so fast. It will take me a while to get it all straight in my head."

Just then the sound of engines could be heard in the distance.

"Looks like your dad's back." Said Tansya turning to Datch.

"Hmm, I suppose I had better go meet him."

"Yes, that sounds like a good idea."

Datch got up and headed down towards one of the out buildings. Dechow's truck came over the roof and landed next to him. Dechow got out.

"Hi Dad."

"Hello Datch."

"Err, I know that you're mad with me. Sorry."

"Datch, annoyed is more the word but I want to know why?"

"We found her dying in the jungle and couldn't leave her to be eaten by the wild animals. So, we saved her."

"Yes, I understand that bit but why did you bring her home."

"Err, it was the IPSF officers, they said that because we had put the Bellatrixian language matrix in her head we had to bring her with us."

"IPSF officers, are you in trouble with the IPSF?"

"Err, No. They were being a bit sort of naughty themselves so we came to an arrangement and Kristina was happy to come with us. So, we had a few drinks with them before we left."

"Naughty? What do you mean?"

"Well, they were using a high-tech scanner to track us in LA and they were not meant to have anything above Earth's Tech level. So, we said that we wouldn't say anything if they didn't."

"What's an LA?"

"It's a city on Earth with a lot of nutty people in it."

"How did you end up there?"

"Well, we parked the Raven in a parking lot and went for ice-cream."

"Just how did you manage to park a starship in the middle of an Earth city without the local authorities noticing?"

"Err, we put a sign on it advertising a new movie. The locals all came and had their photos taken in front while we did some shopping."

"And that's when you ran into the IPSF?"

"Oh, no, that was in the bar when we were having dinner."

Dechow stood looking at his son in disbelief.

"So, what happens now?"

"Well, Widfab has sorted out an implant for her and that will be fitted later this afternoon in the embassy, we have decided that if the others are willing, she can become one of the backing singers."

"And where is she going to live?"

"Well, she will be living with me and Carina to start with and then when she's found her feet and wants to get a place of her own, she can."

"You have thought about this a lot, haven't you?"

"Yes, we had to, me and Carina are responsible for her."

"Hmm..." Dechow looked at his son and was deep in thought for a moment.

"And you're not in trouble with the IPSF?"

"No."

He thought a bit more and then came to a decision.

"OK. fair enough. Just one thing though?"

"What?"

"Why Earth?"

"Ice-cream of course."

"Ice-cream?"

"Yes, we wanted ice-cream. We have brought back lots of different flavours. We got them from the ice-cream parlour in LA. The ice-cream company is going to go nuts when they try them."

"Ok, come on then, you had better introduce me to, Kristina?"

"Yes, Kristina."

They walked up towards the pool.

"A new movie ay?"

"Yes, the city is full of crazy people who will do anything to get on the TV. So, I parked the Raven in full view, put up some signs and gave the parking attendant some of their money stuff who was more than happy to look after it while we went shopping."

"Well, I have to give you credit for style on that one. It sure beats flashing lights in a wood."

By the time they reached the poolside they were both laughing. Carina breathed a sigh of relief when they appeared around the corner of the bar.

'All sorted' Came a voice in her head.

'Good' Said a voice in Datch's

"Dad, this is Kristina." Said Datch as they arrived at the table.

"Hello."

"Hello sir." Said Kristina.

"Just call me Dechow."

"Ok, Dechow."

They sat down and Dechow wanted to know how much Earth had changed since he was there and that made Kristina feel more welcome.

The rest of the morning disappeared and then it was time for Datch and the girls to head to the city. They took Kristina to their house after collecting all their things from the Raven. She was given the larger of the spare rooms to be her bedroom. The she was shown around the house before they went back outside.

Implants.

Datch and Carina fetched their bikes out of the Raven and Kristina got on behind Carina. They slowly moved forwards and then took to the sky. Kristina watched as the ground dropped away beneath them. The last time she was on the bikes it was dark so no one would see them and now it was the middle of the day. It took her a few moments to relax.

"This is cool." She said loudly.

"Yes, it is and you don't have to shout. These helmets have com units built into them." said Carina.

"Oh, sorry."

"Just sit back and enjoy the view." Added Datch's voice in her ear.

"Ok."

She watched as they flew over a small village before crossing over fields full of crops ready to be harvested. Robots could be seen working in the fields and here and there were houses with barns and outhouses. The thing that struck her was the lack of normal roads. Just a couple of freeways heading towards the city and a few small tracks scattered about. When she thought about it why would they need them. Everything could fly.

Below, the fields started to turn to buildings. The bikes slowed down and houses appeared below them spread out with green areas. None of the buildings had been rammed on top of each other like the cities on Earth. Instead, the buildings were spread out with parks and green areas between them. In front of them was the city with its tall glass towers in the corporate area. The spaceport was sitting in the centre surrounded with parks before the multi-story buildings of the inner city took over.

The traffic around the bikes was getting busier now with other vehicles starting to get closer. They were entering the main part of the city. The buildings were two or three stories high now and the bikes started to drop down in between them.

Up ahead was a number of very posh looking buildings with ornate stone work and large golden plaques outside, none of which Kristina could read. To her the letters looked like Aztec hieroglyphics. The bikes dropped down to street level and pulled up outside a somewhat more colourful building.

The building had alternating pure white and yellow steps with bright orange railings leading up to green and golden doors. Above the doors was a large green illuminated gem which pulsed on and off. To the side of it was a sign saying 'Kabab house and night club this way' with an arrow pointing to the alley at the side of the building. Next to the doors was a gold plaque with 'Welly Embassy' stamped on it in Bellatrixian.

Datch and Carina got off the bikes.

"I really need this don't I?" Kristina said slowly getting off the bike.

"Yes, you do and don't worry. It's going to be fine. I promise." said Carina taking her hand.

"Ok." She said reluctantly.

Kristina was feeling very nervous and worried about having something in her head. Nanobots were ok because they were small and she swallowed them like a pill. Therefore, nanobots were like medicine but this was different and she didn't like the idea of it.

Datch led the way through the door. The inside was a large open space with a small seating area at one side with a café. The other side was a long desk with a number of staff members standing at it. Above them hung a green gem that was pulsating. Datch looked at his ring and realised the two were in sync.

A staff member looked up when he heard the door open. He said something to the woman next to him and she went running off up a long staircase at the far end. The man came running over to them.

"Music Warriors, I'm very honoured to meet you." He said bowing.

Datch coughed and looked at him.

"Oh, Err, Sorry. I forgot, no bowing. Please forgive me."

Datch smiled.

"You are forgiven. Just try not to do it again. You have something for us?"

"Oh yes, Music Warrior. My colleague has just gone to fetch the ambassador. He has been given strict instructions from the Minster Prime."

"Just call me Datch please."

"Oh, I couldn't. You're my spiritual leader."

"OK. Just try not to bow too much."

Kristina turned to Carina,

"What's all the bowing about?"

"We are sort of demigods to Welly four. It happened a few months ago. We went to play a couple of gigs and got made demigods."

"Do they do that a lot?"

"No. It was apparently seventy thousand years since they did the last one."

"Oh, and they did it because you played a gig?"

"Sort of. The whole end of darkness thing that we mentioned on the way from Sol three. We'll explain about it later."

Just then a man in a very colourful suit came walking down the stairs flanked with four other staff. He came over to them.

"Music Warriors. It's an honour to meet you." He took a deep bow towards them.

At this point Datch gave up and bowed back.

"Hello, nice to meet you to. Err, you have something for us?"

"Yes, my aid has it here. We have a room set out over there for the procedure. Please follow me."

He led the way across the room to a door at the end of the counter and went in.

The room was tastefully decorated with a large mural on one wall depicting a monastery in the desert with a tall tower in the centre and a green gem on the top. It was so well done that you could almost think you were there. The room had a desk and chairs at one end and seating along the opposite side to the mural. In the centre of the room was a bed with a white sheet over it. The sheet had a bright green gem printed on it.

"OK," said the ambassador, "If the lady would like to lay on the bed."

"Come on." Said Carina, "I'll help you up."

"I'm very nervous."

"Don't be, everyone here has them. It doesn't hurt at all."

Kristina climbed onto the bed. Datch stood on the opposite side to Carina.

"Sorry, but we need to know her surname?" asked the ambassador."

"It's Martínez." Said Kristina.

"Thank you." He turned to Datch.

"The start up memories are from last time you were on Welly four. We thought it was important that they were included."

"Oh, which ones?" asked Datch.

"The bit where you became spiritual leaders and one of your performances and finally a flyby of the pleasure moon."

"You ever thought of going into marketing?"

"No, why do you think I should?"

Datch suddenly realised if he said 'yes', the ambassador was likely to go and get a job selling things.

"No ambassador, I think you're in the right job and you paint a very nice picture of Welly four."

"Thank you, your holiness. Shall we proceed?"

"Yes, please."

The ambassador took the box off of his aid and placed it next to Kristina.

"Lay down please Kristina." he said.

Carina nodded and held her hand as she lay on the bed.

The ambassador pressed the button on the top of the box.

There was a humming noise and Kristina started to feel a fuzzy sensation in her head. Then her mind exploded. The world around her disappeared in a flash of bright light and then she was standing on an alien world watching Datch and Carina along with other people that she recognised as The Pack. They were standing in front of a group of people who were bowing at them. Her mind's eye then shifted and she was at an open-air concert in a natural amphitheatre where the walls lit up with green fire. Then, as that came to an end, she was flying past a moon in a space ship and down below she could see what looked like a water park with a lot of flashing lights that looked like someone was having a really good party there. Slowly she came back to the room. She blinked and turned to Carina.

"Err, that was, err…"

"Just stay still for a few minutes. The implant is still marking connections to your brain. You're going to feel a bit queasy for a few moments."

"I'll get her a drink." Said the ambassador.

"I think we could all do with one." said Datch

"Err, would beer be good?"

"I'll have a Traxsent Starburst please and I think Kristina needs one too." Said Carina.

"And yes, I'll have a beer please ambassador."

He waved at one of the aids who gave a little bow and went running off.

"How are you feeling Kristina?" the ambassador asked.

"Err, A bit light headed and I seem to have a flashing yellow spot in the corner of my eye."

"That's the implant sorting itself out, it will disappear once its happy." he said.

"How long was I dreaming for?"

"Only about five minutes and they were not dreams, they were memories from people who were there. They will stay with you until you either delete them or die."

"I don't understand."

"Don't worry, we'll explain it later in the Barbers." said Carina.

"Yes, just relax and let the implant get to know you. It took me a few hours but I was only five. It will be a lot quicker with you." added Datch.

Kristina started to get up and stopped half way.

"Oh, I feel a bit shaky."

"It will pass. Just try to sit still until the yellow flashing light stops and flashes green three times. It will then disappear."

The aid came back with the drinks and handed them around.

"Thank you for doing this for us." Said Datch.

"No problem. dude. It's a great honour to serve the Music Warriors. I'll be telling my great grandchildren about this day. The day I helped the saviours of the world, my family will be so proud of me."

"I'm glad. You have helped us a lot ambassador."

They helped Kristina off the bed and over to one of the chairs. The ambassador's aids took the box and bed away leaving them with just the ambassador.

Ten minutes later Kristina noticed the light in her eye change from yellow to green and then it vanished.

"The light has stopped flashing." she said.

"Good, now try to read this." Said Datch handing her a piece of paper.

To start with the sheet just looked like a collection of strange lines and squiggles and then, as if by magic, the sheet transformed into text she could read. She looked at it and then at the wall next to the mural. What she thought was a piece of the art work turned out to be a piece about the artist.

"Oh, my god. I can read everything."

The ambassador turned to her,

"Can you understand me, Kristina?"

"Yes, why?"

"Good, because I'm speaking in Wella, my native tongue."

"But it sounds like Bellatrixian."

"Oh wow, I thought it would translate to Portuguese." Said Carina.

"Portuguese isn't in the implants database remember so it's using the one that it knows." Said Datch.

"So, are you saying I can understand any language now?"

"Yes, but you'll hear them as Bellatrixian. The same with the writing, it will translate it all for you automatically. Although sometimes there is a bit of a delay but you'll get used to that."

"Wow. This is incredible."

"OK, before you try to read everything in the building let's see if you can stand up. Just don't move to quickly to start with."

Kristina stood up with Datch and Carina standing on either side of her. She turned and started to move towards they window taking small steps to start with and then increased them to normal steps.

"How are you feeling?" Asked Datch.

"OK, I think. I feel quite normal now. Although my head is still a bit foggy."

"It's only a small trip to the Barbers from here so I think you'll be alright and you can sit down when you get there. The beer will help to."

Datch turned to the ambassador,

"Ambassador, I think we will be off now if that's ok."

"Yes, of course, but before you go would you mind signing this for my wife."

He held out a card.

"Yes, what is your wife's name?"

"Jenna."

Datch put the card on the table and wrote.

'To Jenna. Have a wonderful life and the blessing of the Music Warriors be with you.

PS your husband has helped us out and may you both have many grandchildren. We send our blessings to both of you and your family.

Datch'

He passed it to Carina who also signed it.

She passed the card back to him. He took it and read it.

"Oh, thank you Music Warriors. Thank you."

"You're very welcome."

"Please, let me show you out."

They got up and headed to the door keeping close to Kristina in case she felt faint. They walked across the main reception area towards the main doors and she seemed to be doing fine. They reached the main doors and went outside. Standing by the bikes were a number of aids who seemed to be excited about seeing the machines. As Datch and the girls approached, they stepped to the side and bowed to them. Datch and Carina helped Kristina on to Carina's bike before bowing and getting on the bikes themselves.

"Thanks again ambassador for your help."

"No problem, dudes, keep on partying."

Datch started his bike and Carina followed suit. The aids all stood back and watched as the Music Warriors headed off down the street.

"Err, does that happen all the time?" Asked Kristina.

"What?" Said Carina.

"The bowing and being treated like gods bit."

"No, only with folks from Welly four. Most other fans try to rip our clothes off."

"Oh!"

"Only at the big gigs though. The Barbers Inn is our place and we have our own space there."

"Good, because I'm not sure I'd like having my clothes ripped off by mistake."

"No, that won't happen anyway as we have Timbo."

The bikes started to drop down to street level before coming to a stop next to six other bikes.

"Well, it looks like the gang is here." Said Datch getting off his bike.

Datch and Carina opened their back boxes and got out the bags of gifts for The Pack. Kristina was looking a little nervous, Datch turned to her.

"Kristina, the people inside are our friends. Don't be nervous. We trust them with our lives and have done a number of times."

"OK."

"But before we go in, I'll just want you to do something."

"What?"

Datch thought for a moment and then said

"Think to yourself. What is Bellatrixian Ale?"

"Why?"

"Just try it please?"

"OK."

There was a moments pause and then.

"Oh my god! It's talking to me."

"Yes, if you want to know anything just ask the question in your mind and the implant will give you the answer. So, if they say something you don't understand just ask your implant. OK?"

"Wow, Yes, I will."

With that they walked through the doors into The Barbers Inn.

Jim was at the bar working out his stock and looked up as they came in. He started to point up the stairs and then stopped as he spotted Kristina.

They walked over to the bar.

"Hi Jim, how's it going?"

"Good thanks Datch. Did you have a good honeymoon?"

"Yes, it was quite relaxing."

"We had a lot of fun as well." Added Carina.

"Cool. So, who is this young lady?"

"Jim, this is Kristina."

"Pleased to meet you." said Kristina.

"Pleased to meet you as well. Err, do you sing?"

Datch stepped in before things started to run before, they could walk.

"Maybe, but that's for later. Anyway, we have something for you when you come up stairs."

"So, what you drinking?"

"We'll have the normal. Kristina, do you want beer, wine or something else?"

"Err, wine please."

"White, Red?"

"Err, a sweet white please."

"No probs, I'll bring them up to you."

"Thanks Jim."

They headed to the stairs and removed the chain with a sign on it saying 'VIP's ONLY'. Datch and the girls went up the stairs putting the sign back as they went.

The Pack were sitting at the table chatting when Tank looked up.

"Guys, they're back!" he said standing up.

The others all turned around.

"Hi folks." Said Datch and then there was a round of hellos.

"So, who is this then?" Asked Tish looking at Kristina,

"This is Kristina, she is sort of part of the family now. please take it easy with her as she only got her implant an hour ago and she is still getting used to it." Said Carina.

"Hello and welcome." Said Fred.

"Let me introduce everyone." Said Datch who then proceeded to go around everyone in turn.

"So, where are you from?" asked Peebop.

"I'm from Earth."

"Earth, where is Earth?" asked Clax.

"Sol three." Said Carina.

"Sol three?" asked Dapo.

"The one where the ice-cream came from."

"I thought that world hadn't made contact yet?" said Clax.

"It hasn't."

"Well, how the Jaxx did you end up there?"

"We wanted ice-cream."

"So, let me get this right, you were on honeymoon and decided to go to a planet that hasn't made contact yet for ice-cream and ended up coming back with one of the locals."

"Yes, and we also have a lot of tubs of ice-cream in the Raven."

"You do? How many?" said Rosey taking a sudden interest.

"Thirty-five new flavours for you to try." Added Datch.

"Wow. When can we try them?"

"I'll bring a couple down tomorrow if you like?"

"That sounds very good." Said Rosey who was now planning on bringing her special spoon with her. No one was sure why it was a special spoon as it came from a very normal pack of spoons and looked like a normal spoon. But apparently it was special.

Just at that point Jim came up stairs with the drinks.

"Thanks Jim." Said Datch as Jim put the drinks down.

"So how did you meet Kristina then?" asked Clax.

"We helped her out and she wanted to come with us."

"Yes, and she can sing." said Carina joining in.

"What did you do, hold auditions at the ice-cream factory?" Said Dapo.

"No, not quite." said Datch and gave Dapo a stare.

"Err, sorry."

"Ok. The easiest way is for us to tell you about our honeymoon. Then all your questions will be answered."

"And you get presents halfway through." Added Carina.

"We do?" said Hagger.

"Yes." said Datch.

"This should be good, Jim, get another round of drinks for everyone and can we have some buckets of fried Hacks and fries."

"Sure, I'll grab a drink myself to. I'd like to hear all about this myself."

"Err, sorry, but could someone tell me where the bathroom is?" asked Kristina.

"Sure, I'll take you. I need to use it myself." said Tish.

The two of them got up and headed down the stairs following Jim.

"Datch. What are you planning?"

"Nothing as such. We were just thinking that she would make a good addition as a backing singer. We have male voices at the moment. Adding a female voice will balance the sound better."

"Are you sure she can sing?"

"Yes, we did karaoke with her." said Carina,

"I recorded it. Just hit accept folks." Said Datch.

He transferred a copy of it to everyone. Fred had already watched a couple of minutes of it by the time Datch had gone around the table.

"I'll say this, she does have a good voice on her."

"Guys, Tish and Kristina are coming back." said Carina.

"Please watch it and then we'll discuss it tomorrow if that's OK?" said Datch.

"Ok."

Jim came back up the stairs along with another member of staff carrying their drinks. Tish and Kristina were following behind them.

"Food will be about ten mins folks." he said pulling up a chair.

"Where do we start, hmm, Luyten. After the wedding we decided to go to Luyten to chill out."

"Is that the one with the pink sand?" asked Rosey.

"Yes, so we were chilling by the pool when we decided we wanted ice-cream..." Datch continued to tell the story along with Carina and they had just got to where they saved Kristina when the food turned up.

"What are Hacks?" asked Kristina.

"Try asking your implant." said Datch.

"Oh, yes." she said.

She stopped and looked into space for a moment.

"Oh, they are large chickens." she said with a big smile on her face.

The story was paused for a few moments while the food was sorted out and then continued.

"So, you were in the jungle carrying Kristina through the undergrowth." Said Fred whilst eating a Hacks wing.

Datch and Carina carried on with the tale and now Kristina started to add her bits in as it progressed.

They reached the part with the drug lord and Fred looked at Datch.

"What? We did ask nicely."

"And you really expected him to go?"

"Err, well, No."

"Anyway, they pretty much killed themselves. After all, the bullets just kept bouncing back at them."

"Yes, and then they tried to blow us up. So, it was self-defence." Added Carina with a grin.

"They attacked us with three of their aircraft so I pressed the fire button."

"And?" said Fred.

"Well, there were a lot of little bits of aircraft all over the place."

"You do realise that you were never in danger. Don't you?"

"Oh, we knew. That's what made it fun."

"Anyway…" said Datch and continued.

Another round of drinks came out and they got to the LA part.

"Ok, so while we were in the market, we thought it would be good to get you all gifts."

"OK, cool." Said Rosey.

"Carina, do want to start with your bag."

"Sure." She reached in her bag and pulled out the pink dolphin.

"Tank, we thought you would like this?"

"What is it?"

"It's a dolphin." Said Kristina.

"It's cute, I'll put it was my pink teddy."

"And for you Fred," she handed him a heated boot warmer.

"What is it?"

"It warms your boots up. We thought it may come in handy next time you go skiing in Traxsent."

The rest of The Pack burst out laughing.

"Ok, Ok. I'm sure it will come in handy." he said smiling.

Carina worked her way through the bag and then it was Datch's turn.

"OK, what have I got? Ah yes, Clax."

He pulled out a book and handed it to him.

"It's about the ancient humans."

"I'll enjoy that. Thanks."

He reached in and went to pull at another book and then realised Jep was missing.

"Where's Jep?"

"Oh, he's got a meeting with his publisher and said he would be down later."

"OK, Jim, it took a bit of thinking about but we thought you would like a proper Earth tankard. They drink out of them in some places so we were told."

He fetched it out and handed it to him.

"Wow, I'll put that behind the bar on display. Thanks, Datch."

Datch finished handing out the presents.

"So, what happened next?"

"We went to the beach for a paddle. Before heading to the ice-cream parlour."

"I bet it was really cool." Said Tish.

"Yes, it had pictures of ice-creams with cakes and waffles in various shapes on the walls and a big display case full of ice-cream."

"Oh, wow, what did you do?"

"He started drooling." said Carina and they all laughed.

The shop was then described in great detail along with the ice-creams.

"So, they put biscuits in the ice-cream?" said Jim thoughtfully.

"Yes, sometimes. We had a really nice sweet in Roswell. Look."

Datch pulled up an image on his vid and showed it to Jim.

"Wow, that does look good. Is it ok for my chef to have a look?"

"Sure, maybe he could try making us one. The biscuits are wafer thin and it has cream that is whisked up on top with a flaky stick of chocolate in it. It also has a cookie texture to the Ice-cream."

Jim got up and waved at the bar. Two minutes later the chef was standing next to Datch looking at the vid com.

He had a very thoughtful look on his face.

"I can give it a go if you like?"

"Cool, that would be great."

"Could you send me a copy of the images and the scan of it please?"

"Sure."

Datch pressed a few buttons and the chef's vid com beeped.

"It might take a while to work it out though."

"Ok, Thanks. If you can do it, can we have six of them?"

"I might make them slightly different to work out the best way of doing it, if that's ok?"

"Cool."

With that the chef left them and Datch carried on with the story.

Another round of drinks later, they finally got to Luyten and then home.

"Wow, quite an adventure you had."

"Yes, it was very relaxing." said Datch.

"Well, I had better get on. I need to see what the chef is doing." said Jim getting up.

"Ok, see you in a bit." said Fred.

Jim left them and Fred turned to Kristina.

"So, Kristina. It looks like you're stuck with us."

"Stuck. No, I'm loving every minute. It's like an endless adventure."

"From what Datch has told us, you can sing?" said Peebop.

"Err," she looked at Datch. He nodded and smiled.

"Datch said I can but I'm not sure."

"Did you show her?" he said looking at Datch.

"Err, no. She didn't have her implant when I recorded it."

"Show me what?" said Kristina looking concerned.

"The karaoke on Luyten. I recorded it with my implant. Now you have yours, you can watch it."

"Oh, like we do on Earth with our phones you mean."

"Sort of. I'll make a box appear in your mind just think accept and then you can view it."

"Wow, you can do that?"

"Yes, are you ready?"

Kristina nodded and then a smile appeared on her face and then a frown followed by a smile that got bigger.

Datch looked around the table. They were all watching Kristina for her reactions, that is apart from Hagger who was playing a game on his vid com. Datch was hoping they would accept her into the group. He thought she could bring a lot to The Pack but it would depend on the next few days.

There was a shout from down stairs and Datch looked over the balcony. The chef had just come out of the kitchen with a tray of glasses filled with ice-cream. Jim went over to have a look at them and said something to him. The chef nodded and headed along the back of the bar before coming up the stairs.

"Do I really sing like that?" said Kristina coming out of her trance and looking at Datch.

"Yes." said Datch.

"I wobbled a bit at the beginning."

"Yes, but that was your first time on the stage." said Carina.

"I thought it was very good for a first time." added Rosey.

"Thank you."

Just at that point the chef arrived at the table and placed the tray down in front of Datch. He was looking very pleased with himself.

"Datch, what do you think of these?" he asked.

Datch looked at them. The glasses were nearly the right shape, the ice-cream was layered with chocolate coloured cream and chocolate syrup, The whole thing was then topped with a swirl of whipped cream and to finish it off, two chocolate flakes had been inserted along with a large thin wafer.

"They look great." Datch said picking up a spoon.

He dug the spoon into one of the sundaes removing a section of the ice-cream and placed it in his mouth and savoured the taste for a moment before getting another spoon full and offering it to Carina. She took it and put it in her mouth.

'I think it's pretty close.' Came a voice in her head.

She let the ice-cream melt in her mouth before answering.

'Yes, not bad at all,'

"Well?" said the chef eager to get an answer.

"It's pretty dam perfect. Maybe if you put a bit more chocolate cookie in it for added texture. But that's all I can think of."

"Yes, I agree." Added Carina.

"That's good, try that one there. I've done that with them." said the chef pointing to the two on the far side of the tray.

Datch put his spoon in and felt a bit more resistance. He picked it out and put it in his mouth. Carina took a spoonful as well.

"Hmm… Yes, that's it." said Datch.

"Yes, I think so. Kristina, what do you think?" Carina said passing her a spoon. She took a spoonful.

The chef looked like an expectant farther.

"Yes, tastes like it." she agreed.

"So, them at the back, yes?"

"Yes, the two at the back are spot on. The rest are pretty close as well. I think they need to be slightly wider glasses and a little deeper. Sort of a wide cone shape inside." Said Datch.

"Good, I'll go and try some more glasses."

"You did a great job with them. Thank you." said Datch.

"Yes, good work." Added Carina.

"Thanks" said Kristina.

"Thank you. Please enjoy them."

The chef left them with the tray of sundaes and went down stairs with a big grin on his face.

Everyone at the table grabbed a spoon to try the new dessert. They all dug in and soon the glasses were all empty.

"Well, that's an alien import I really like." Said Peebop licking his lips.

"Kristina, do you fancy a game?" asked Rosey.

"You mean Solar Ball?"

Rosey looked at Datch and Carina.

"What, we had a thirty six hour trip and we got a bit bored on Earth." said Datch.

"I'm in," said Tish.

"Me too." said Carina.

"Ok, me too." said Kristina.

"Kristina, take it easy down there, remember, you have just got your implant. If you feel lightheaded, stop, ok?" said Datch

"Ok." she said and followed the girls down the stairs.

After they had gone Datch turned to the others.

"So, do you think she will be ok?"

"Can I suggest that we take her to the studio and see how she gets on." said Fred.

"Yes, but it's not just if she can sing but if she fits in with the group." added Clax.

"Granted." Said Fred.

"When are we gigging again?" asked Datch

"In a couple of weeks, we're doing the Barbers first and then the capital four days later." Said Fred.

"Ok, that gives you time to get to know her."

"Don't forget Jep."

"Yes, where is he, I thought he was coming?"

"I'll give him a call."

Fred picked up his vid com and called Jep. It turned out he was tied up with his publisher and was hoping to be on his way shortly.

Then suddenly the table turned into a ledge on the side of a cliff that had a very large bird's nest with a number one sitting on it. The rest of the room turned into a craggy pit surrounded by steep cliffs with rocks jutting out. Giant birds started to fly around the bar and one landed on Rosey's chair. Hagger jumped out of his skin as he was playing his game at the time and hadn't noticed the game start. Then a ball came flying up from below and hit the bird's beak before going in the nest.

Datch turned to watch the girls. They seemed to be getting on well. Datch hoped that they would accept Kristina because if they didn't, he had no idea what to do with her. He was responsible for her being here and had to make sure she was alright. He let out a sigh.

"What's up?" asked Clax.

"Nothing, I just want Kristina to be ok. That's all."

"I suppose you're finding out what it's like to have kids." said Peebop.

"How would you know? You guys don't have kids." Said Dapo.

"I do." said Peebop.

"You do?" said Fred turning to him.

Everyone turned to look at Peebop.

"What, it was a long time ago in a star system a long way away."

"Really?" said Tank.

"Err, well, it was nine hundred light years away."

"And?" Said Clax.

They were all staring at him.

"Ok, I had a relationship with a woman from Ionus three for about a year."

"So?" asked Fred.

"Well, we got a bit err, eager and she forgot her inhibitor was turned off."

"It was?" said Clax.

"Yes, so I have a son."

"How come you never told us?"

"I don't have any contact with them. She sends me a picture or two every now and again but that's about it. I'm not even sure if he knows who I am."

The bird took to the air just as another ball shot across the table missing the nest by about a metre.

"How old is he?" asked Tank.

"Two hundred and six, I think."

"Oh, it was a long time ago!"

They sat in silence for a moment and then Fred spoke.

"Well, that sure beats bringing an alien home from your honeymoon."

"Can we see him?"

"Sure."

Peebop picked up his vid com and called up a number of pictures.

"He's got orange hair." Said Tank.

"Yes, he takes after his mum."

"So, have you ever wanted to go and see him?"

The bird that had just taken off landed next to Fred and looked at him sideways as if it was debating having him for lunch.

"I did for a few years while he was growing up but after he moved out from his mum's I sort of stopped."

"Oh. Maybe if we are gigging in that system at some point, we can call in so you can see him."

"It would be nice."

"So, what happened with you and his mum?"

"I was young and working my way across the stars. I was only going to be there for a few weeks so we had some fun and then we found out she was expecting. So, I stopped for a year but we were not getting on well at all, so I left."

"Was that it, didn't you try and take him with you?"

"No, I just wanted to explore the universe and party a lot. So, he stayed with her." he sighed.

A holographic ball hit the celling and landed in the nest.

"Well, the girls are having fun." said Fred changing the subject.

Carina and Tish were the green team and Rosey and Kristina were the blue. They were all having fun and Kristina was laughing along with them.

"Yes, it looks like they are."

They sat watching them play and by the time they came back to the table it was early evening and Kristina was looking tired. It had been a long couple days for all three of them and especially for Kristina, what with coming to a new world and having her implant fitted.

Datch called his mum to sort out some food and then arranged to meet the rest of them at the studio the following lunchtime. They sat and finished their drinks before getting ready to go. Jep still hadn't turned up so Datch told Fred to say 'hi'.

The three of them headed outside and mounted the bikes. Kristina looked up just in time to see a cargo ship coming into land at the spaceport. The ship slowed almost to a stop before turning itself around and then dropping down behind the buildings. Carina started the bike's engines and followed Datch as he took to the air.

They arrived back at the ranch just as Tansya was setting the table out in the veranda. They landed outside of their house and then walked across to the ranch.

"Hi, mum." Said Datch walking up.

"Hi, Datch. How did you get on?"

"Good. Kristina's got her implant and is now a citizen of Bellatrix and we're taking her to the studio tomorrow to see how she does."

"How are you feeling Kristina?"

"OK, I think. This implant is sort of cool."

At that point Dechow came out of the bar with a beer in his hand.

"Hi folks."

"Hi dad." said Datch and the girls both followed suit

"I'll go and get the food." said Tansya

"I'll help." said Carina

"I'll come too." added Kristina.

The girls went inside and Datch fetched a beer from the bar.

"So, how did Kristina get on?"

"OK dad. She's got her implant now and the gang seems to like her."

"Good. So, what do you have planned?"

"Well, I'm taking the Raven to the spaceport service area tomorrow to get her refuelled and then we're going to head to the studio to see if Kristina will work singing backing vocals."

"So, when is your next gig?"

"In a couple of weeks at the Barbers and then we're off to the capital."

"Are you taking the Raven?"

"No, we'll take a transport. It will save a lot of messing about sorting out parking for the Raven. Anyway, there is a hotel there we like. So, we'll spend a couple of days there."

At that point the girls came out with plates and various bowls of food. Tansya had made Jaxx slices in a sauce, Kella fries and a salad to go with them. Carina was carrying the plates and gave them out to everyone along with the cutlery while Kristina and Tansya placed the dishes of food in the centre of the table. Kristina sat down looking at the others.

"We don't stand on ceremony here Kristina. Just tuck in." said Dechow grabbing a number of Jaxx slices with the serving tongs and placing them on his plate.

"What is it?"

"That there is Jaxx meat in a Rena berry sauce, Kella fries and that is a green leaf salad with a few sliced peppers thrown in to add colour."

"It all looks great."

She took some of each dish and placed it on her plate and they all started eating.

"So, Kristina. Have Datch and Carina been explaining what your implant can do?" asked Dechow.

"Yes, and they keep showing me new things. So far, I've learnt to ask it things and how to play videos in my head."

"Good, I think you mean vids. Video is an Earth term."

"Well, Datch sent me a vid that he had recorded and told me how to play it."

"Ah, now that is a recorded memory. Vids are recorded using vid bots or a holo cam and a recorded memory is stored using the implant."

"Oh, so that was Datch's memory?"

"Yes, it was."

"Wow. That's cool."

"I take it by the way you're walking around that you have been given nanobots?"

"Yes, Datch gave them to me before we got to Luyten."

"Did they tell you that you'll live longer now?"

"Yes, they explained it to me when we left Earth."

"Good." He looked at Datch and smiled.

"This is a great place you have here." She said turning around to look at everything. It was then she noticed them.

"We like it." Said Tansya.

"Oh my god! There are two moons." Kristina said looking into the darkening sky.

"There are three in fact. The other one will be up in the early morning. The ones you can see there are the smaller two. Didn't you see them on the way down?" asked Dechow.

"No Dad, the lanes were busy and they were pretty much on the other side of the planet."

"That's a shame they look much better from space. What about the space stations?"

"Err, I think I was too busy looking at the ships in front of us. It was all very exciting seeing so many spaceships and my new world from space."

"Well, if you become part of The Pack, you'll be seeing even more planets." said Carina.

"Yes, a lot more." added Datch.

"Well, I hope they like my singing."

"They liked what they have seen so far and you seem to be getting on well with everyone." said Datch smiling.

"Yes, we had a lot of fun this afternoon." added Carina.

"Yes, it was fun."

"Let's move over to the sofas. I'll go and clear the pots away." said Tansya.

"I'll help." said Kristina keen to make a good impression.

"Ok. Thanks."

The women took the pots inside and Datch and Dechow got a round of drinks from the bar. Five minutes later they were all sitting outside having a drink, looking out across the fields towards the city.

"What's that over there?" said Kristina pointing up into the sky.

"That is one of the space stations." Said Dechow.

"Wow. It looks so big."

"It's about the size of a city and is sitting forty-three thousand kilometres above the equator."

"We'll take you there at some point. But for now, I think we should have a couple more drinks after these and then head to bed." said Carina.

"Yes, sounds good." said Datch.

They sat and talked more about Earth and what Kristina thought of Bellatrix five. The evening turned to night and Datch, Carina and Kristina headed back to their house. Carina introduced her to the computer that ran the house and got her registered as living there. Then they headed off to bed.

Kristina lay there in her new bed looking out the window at the stars and the tiny lights moving across the sky that were the ships coming and going at the spaceport. She tried to take stock of what had happened to her.

She was now for all intense and purposes an alien to even her own world. Her own world, this was her world now not Earth. And so far, it had been alright. Datch and Carina's friends had accepted her and she now had an implant. She decided to ask it how many worlds were like this one and the implant popped the answer into her head. Her mind went back to her mum, what would she say. She would be amazed, that's for sure and pleased that she was safe. She was not sure what she would think about the implant or the fact that she was now destined to live for seven thousand years. seven thousand years, that's a long time. What would she see? Her mind started to drift and then she fell asleep.

A New Recruit.

The next morning, she woke up and looked around the room. It took her a few moments to think where she was. Bellatrix. She looked across to the window and to the light green sky outside. She got up and headed over to it. The desert was off to the right and rolling sands could be seen disappearing into the distance. Down below, Datch and Carina were sitting in the garden having breakfast. Kristina got up and after a quick shower went down stairs to join them.

"Good morning." She said as she walked out of the patio doors holding a cup of coffee that the kitchen had been nice enough to supply.

"Morning." Said Carina.

"Did you sleep well?" asked Datch.

"Yes thanks."

"We guessed as much, it's almost lunch time." said Datch.

"Is it? How long was I sleep?"

"About twelve hours." Said Carina.

"Oh, I don't normally need that much."

"It will be because your implant was installed yesterday and the time difference from Luyten to here." answered Carina.

"Anyway, we have to make a move soon. I've got to drop the Raven off at the spaceport to be refuelled before we head to the studio. Then we can see how you sound on backing vocals." added Datch.

"We're going to the spaceport?" Kristina said smiling.

"Yes, but we won't be walking through the main section. The Raven is going to the servicing area. We just leave via the gate at the side and go back a few hours later when she's been refuelled."

"Oh, I was hoping to see more aliens."

"You might. They get their ships refuelled there as well. In fact, you may see more there than in the main concourse. The cargo ship crews won't normally bother going planet side. Time equals credits for them." Said Carina.

"Yes, they like a quick turnround." added Datch.

"Cool."

They finished their coffees and headed to the Raven ready for the trip to the city.

Datch flew the Raven up and joined the main flow of ships heading for the spaceport. Datch told Yuland control that they were booked into the service area for refuelling and got clearance to land there. As the ship flew towards the city Kristina got a much better view as they were much higher up than she had been on the bikes.

The city was almost circular in shape apart from an area to the south that stuck out making the city look top heavy. The spaceport sat in the centre of the city surrounded by parks and a large lake to the south.

The city itself was split into sections with the corporate area to the south. Government buildings along with libraries and the power plant to the east. To the west was the retail section with shops and bars. And finally, to the north were hotels, museums and the sport stadium.

As you moved out of the inner city, the buildings gave way to the housing that started off as three or four story buildings which as the city spread out dropped down to two story complexes and finally turned into a collection of one or two story houses or villas in the suburbs.

To Kristina it looked like it was very ordered, almost regimental in structure with its clear and very defined areas. She thought it must have taken a lot of planning to make it that way, it made logical sense and also made it look like a work of art. It was as if an artist had walked in a government office and said 'here, I have this design for a city' and they said 'ok we'll build it'. They headed towards the city's heart, the spaceport.

The spaceport was a massive structure with a complex of landing pads and docking portals attached to a large semi-circular building in the centre. Some of the pads had shuttles and small inter-stellar liners sitting on them. To the side of the large building was a number of landing pads with cargo ships sitting on them. They had an army of robots who were unloading and loading cargo along with servicing and repairing the ships. The Raven dropped down towards the service area.

Yuland control guided them to pad thirty-two. Datch brought the Raven in for a soft landing and shut the engines down. They got up and headed out of the ship and into the service area. At the bottom of the ramp a service droid was waiting for them.

Kristina looked at it. It was a sort of mechanical human shape but was very short and wide with a battered looking casing. It also had four arms instead of two, very chunky legs and its head was integrated into its upper body.

"Good morning, sir. How can I be of assistance?" it said.

"Hi. Can you refuel the ship and check the shield emitters please?"

"Yes sir. Do you wish it to be decontaminated?"

Datch thought for a moment.

"I think it should be good but if you could quick scan to check and if needed, please do it. Thanks."

"It will take approximately five hours sir; we are quite busy at the moment."

"No problem. We will be back late in the afternoon anyway."

"Please note sir, parking charges will be applied after eight hours."

"OK, thanks."

The service droid turned and headed off to one of the other ships. Datch led the way to a set of steps leading down to a covered walkway that ran bellow the landing pads and took them towards a building at the end.

Kristina was looking up though the clear roof at the ships as they walked along. One of the ships looked like it had been hit by gun fire as part of its tail section was peppered with holes.

"What happened to that one?" she asked looking at it.

"Most likely got caught in a meteor storm. They can shred your outer hull if you don't have your shields up." Said Datch.

"Have you ever had that happened to you?"

"No, the Raven is a more advanced ship and has auto shielding. Therefore, the shield comes on automatically when danger is detected. Most of the cargo ships tend to be the cheaper end of the market."

"Oh."

There was an alien standing at the back of one of the ships watching the bots load cargo into the hold. It was human in shape, slightly taller than normal, its skin was a yellowish with a brown dappled look and its hair was a reddish colour. It was marking off the crates on a vid com as the cargo was loaded.

"What is that alien?"

"Just look at him and ask your implant to identify lifeform."

Kristina did and the implant told her that he was a Carmarian from the fourth planet of the Betelgeuse star system.

"Can it do that for anything?"

"For most things, yes. The only exceptions are anything to IPSF stuff. That information is omitted for security reasons."

"Oh wow."

She started looking at all the ships and any other aliens that she spotted. Asking her implant about just about everything she could see.

They arrived at the building and Datch turned down towards a security gate. A camera was above it on the wall with a scanner mounted underneath. There was a blue button marked with 'exit'. Datch walked up to it and pressed the button. A light came on and a voice said 'Please wait. Verifying ID's.' There was a slight pause and then the gate opened. It led into a corridor then exited onto the street outside. The three of them walked out of the far end and onto a road that led up to the spaceport's main entrance. They headed across the street towards the parks and into the sunshine. Every now and again a ship's shadow would pass over them.

As they entered the park Kristina was looking down at all the brightly coloured plants, fancy palms and tropical shrubs. Datch led the way to a transit point. The transit system was inside tubes mounted on tall steel supports that went across the park and into the city beyond. Inside Kristina could see carriages traveling along at very high speeds.

They arrived at the transit point and headed up the steps. The platform area had a separate tube connecting it to the main network. Three separate carriages were waiting at the platform and the doors of the front one opened as they approached it. Kristina noticed another camera with a scanner attached to it above the door.

"Does everywhere have cameras?" she asked.

"No, they are only used for security and payment purposes. This one here will scan our ID's and then charge the lead person for the transit cost. In this case Datch." said Carina.

"Does it cost a lot?"

"No, to get to the transit point near Tanks is about a credit each."

They walked into the carriage. It had twenty seats inside set out with two rows of five on each side. They sat down and Datch told the carriage where they were going. After a few moments the carriage started to accelerate rapidly before joining the main transit tube system.

"I'm going to have to get a job. Aren't I?" said Kristina.

"Well, if you can sing in harmony with the others, you will be making credits that's for sure." said Datch.

"How much does it pay?"

"Well, the gig at the Barbers makes us about five hundred credits each as we do it more for fun than anything else but, the big gigs like the one in two weeks time will make us around a hundred and twenty-five thousand each per night and we do two nights." said Carina.

"Just so I can understand. That's two hundred and fifty thousand each so, how much does a beer cost?"

"Hmm, about a credit to a credit and a half." Said Datch.

"You make a lot then?"

"Well, a normal person earns around sixty thousand a year but remember the year is two Earth years."

"And you make double that in one night."

"Yes." said Datch with a grin.

The transit tube started to slow down and then left the main tube before coming to a stop at another platform. This transit point was surrounded by two story housing. They walked down the steps and into the street below. It took them another five minutes to walk to Tanks.

When they arrived, there were a number of bikes outside and a truck.

"It looks like we're last." said Datch walking up to a light red door with a yellow flower painted on it.

The door opened and there was the sound of laughing coming from within. Kristina followed Datch and Carina inside. They headed through to the rear garden. The Pack were all there including Jep.

"Hi all." Said Datch walking out into the garden.

They all turned to look at him and said hello. Afterwards Datch called Jep over.

"Hi Jep. This is Kristina."

"Hello Kristina. Welcome to Bellatrix."

"Thank you."

Datch turned to the others.

"Let's get a beer and then get started, shall we?"

They all grabbed a drink and started to head inside.

"Where is the studio?" asked Kristina.

"In the front room." said Carina.

They went into the studio which was also Tank's spare room and took their places on the make shift stage. Kristina stood and waited.

"Ok, Kristina. If you stand there and listen, we will do Star Lovers. It's sort of the song that made us. Then we'll get you to stand next to Tank and Fred and join in on the second run. Ok?"

"Err, ok." she said looking worried and nervous about doing it.

"Don't worry, we don't expect you to know the words just try to get the harmony."

He turned to Tish and nodded. Star Lovers played and Kristina watched trying to remember the chorus lines. The main issue was she was not only using an alien language but was now about to try and sing it in harmony with others.

The song finished and Datch turned to her.

"Ok, your turn."

She walked over to Tank and Fred.

"We've put a vid screen up with the chorus on so you can just follow it." said Fred trying to put her at ease.

"Right, let's do it."

They started to play and then the first chorus came in. Kristina was a little out of time but was in tune ish. Then the second chorus. This time she was in time but still a little shaky. Each time she was a bit closer. They decided to go through the song few times and see if she improved. Then on the fourth run through she finally got it and her voice came into sync with the others.

"Ok, one more time and I'll record this one." said Datch.

They went for it and Kristina sang her heart out. The rings on Datch's and Carina's fingers energised and the room was filled with a green glow.

"Let's have a look then." said Datch and turned to the vid screen. They stood and watched the replay. There was no doubting the fact that Kristina was adding harmony to the chorus line. She just needed a bit more practice.

"OK. Let's do Supernova." Said Datch.

They went through five songs in total which took up most of the afternoon after which they retired to the back garden.

They had just finished their first beer outside when Datch suggested Carina should show Kristina the pool area out the front.

After they had left Datch turned to the others.

"So, folks, what do you think?"

"Well, she can sing." said Fred.

"Yes, and she does seem to add something to the mix." added Dapo.

Datch looked at them.

"Guys, this is a big step for us. We have been The Pack now for seven years. I want to know if we should give her a go? Don't let me and Carina just say yes. This is a new member of The Pack's family in waiting. If you have any doubts then say so."

"Well, I like her." said Rosey.

"Me too." Said Tish.

"OK. Guys. Do we give her a go?" asked Datch.

He looked at each of them in turn. They all nodded one after another.

"Ok, We'll give her a few weeks and see how she gets on. We'll have another session at the weekend and in the meantime, myself and Carina will teach her our other songs, well the chorus bits anyway. The Barbers gig is what two weeks?"

"Just under." Said Fred.

"We'll try her out then. ok?"

"Ok, but only if she's ready." said Fred.

"Right, I'll get Carina to bring her back in."

'You can bring her back now. They said yes.' Came a voice in Carina's head.

'Cool, we're on our way.' Carina answered back.

Datch turn to the others.

"OK, they are on their way."

"You still have the telepathy thing going on then?" asked Clax.

"Yes, but we know how to control it now. So, we won't be answering our own questions or finishing each other's sentences unless we want to."

"Good, because that was doing our head's in at the joining." Said Tank.

"So, what's next?" Asked Peebop.

"I think we can write another song or two about Arcaneus. I'm also hoping that we can use some of the Earth music. Some of their songs were really good."

"Sounds good. Are we doing that here or at the ranch?"

"The ranch sounds like a good plan. We have more room there to work on them and we can get a few ideas down. I'll talk to Dad."

Just then the door opened and Carina and Kristina walked in. Datch turned to Kristina.

"Kristina, we have just had a bit of a chat while Carina was showing you the pool area. We discussed you becoming part of the band and if you are prepared to work at it, we'll be happy for you to join us doing backing vocals. So, what do you say?"

"Thank you, I would love to."

"Cool, Welcome to The Pack."

There was a general round of welcomes followed by another round of drinks and then everyone had some food. The men spread out around the garden and the girls took over the main table.

Datch sat in the deckchair next to Tank eating a burger when his vid com beeped. He fetched it out of his pocket and looked at it. There was a message from the spaceport service controller saying that the Raven was ready to be collected. He looked over to the girls who were deep in conversation.

"Carina, Kristina, we're going to have to go shortly. The Raven's ready." he said.

"Ok. We'll just finish our drinks then we'll be ready." replied Carina.

Tank turned to Datch.

"What's it like having two women in the house instead of one?" he asked.

"Err, everything takes longer."

"Longer?"

"Yes, instead of Carina just forgetting things and me having to fetch them, Kristina does it as well and has to go back for them. So, longer."

"At least they're both adults and not kids or you would be running around all day."

"Yeh, I suppose so. Still, it's nice having Kristina around. She takes things at face value and therefore gives a whole new perspective to any conversation."

"I expect that's because she's still getting use to the way we live. I'm sure she'll change a bit when she finds her feet in our society." said Clax joining in.

"Yes, but it's seeing the wonder and amazement in her face when she see's things for the first time. We forget how wonderful our world is and she is showing it to me and Carina."

"I never thought of it like that." Said Clax.

"Like what?" said Carina walking up.

"Oh, I was just saying about how Kristina sees the wonder in everything."

"She does, doesn't she." Said Carina thinking about it. "Anyway, we're ready to go when you are."

Datch downed his drink and then got up.

"Ok folks, we'll see you at the ranch this weekend. Do you guys want to stop over?"

"Sure, if it's, ok?" said Fred.

"I'll talk to Dad, oh and bring your kit with you."

"OK, dude." Said Peebop.

The three of them left and headed to the spaceport via the transit system. Fifteen minutes later they arrived at the Raven.

Datch accepted the costs and they boarded the ship. They headed to the cockpit and Datch sat down double checking the systems. Carina turned to Kristina.

"So, Kristina. We need you to learn the chorus lines for the songs but, don't worry, we have a plan."

"What's that?" asked Kristina.

"Well, if we play the songs over and over to you then hopefully you should pick them up quite quickly."

"Ok, when do I start?"

"Tomorrow."

The Raven lifted off and headed back towards the ranch. The trip only took a few minutes and Datch brought the Raven into land on the landing pad near the barn.

As they left the ship Datch went over to a grill and pressed some buttons on a small panel next to it. The grill slid open and he fetched out a long thick power cable with heavy duty power connector on one end. He dragged it over to the Raven and pressed a button on a small panel mounted on the underside. A hatch opened and Datch lifted up the connector and plugged it in. There was a beep from the ships panel and another one from the panel at the grill. Datch checked the locking system to make sure the cable was secure and then turned to follow the girls over to their house.

When they got there a small parcel had arrived for Datch. He picked it up and went inside. He sat down and opened the parcel. Inside was a vid com with a carry case and charging system.

"Kristina?" he said.

She stuck her head around the door that led into the kitchen.

"I've got something for you."

She came walking over with Carina following.

"Me and Carina were talking last night and thought you would need this."

He handed her the box with the vid com in.

"Oh wow, Thank you so much. This is a vid com like the one you use, isn't it?"

"Yes, now press the power button and then it will want to pair with your implant."

"So, like this?"

She pressed the small button on the side and the screen lit up. The screen was displaying a pairing button on it.

"OK, so what do I do?"

"Think pair with vid com and look at it. Then, when the button turns green press it and then a box will appear in your mind asking you to confirm the connection. Accept it and the vid com will initialise."

She did and the vid com beeped and then said connected.

"Ok, So, how do I know what it's number is?"

"Number?"

"Yes, for people to call me."

"Oh, no, it doesn't have a number as such but uses your personal ID. Remember when we said about the implant being used for ID. It came with an ID number built into it. The security gate at the spaceport scanned it without you realising, as did the transit system. When you buy things in shops or bars the sales registers link to your implants ID and ask you to accept the charges."

"So, everything goes through the implant?"

"Well, anything security or financially related. You can also give your ID number to people by looking at their vid com and think send ID. You won't see the actual ID number as it is over a thousand characters long. Their vid com will just prompt them to accept it and when they do your name will pop up on the display for them to confirm it."

"Ok. So, if I look at your vid com and think send ID, my name should appear?"

"Yes, try it with mine." said Carina.

She did and Carina's vid com beeped. Sure enough, the display said accept and after Carina hit accept and Kristina's name appeared on the display and then Carina hit the confirm button.

"OK, that's done. Now do Datch's." said Carina.

She did and Datch accepted and confirmed it.

"Do you have to do the same to me?" she asked.

"No, if you look at your vid com it will be displaying our names in the directory list."

She looked at it for a moment.

"Top button on the left. Looks like a number of wavy lines."

“Oh, I see it.”

She pressed it and Datch and Carina’s names appeared on the display.

“Cool.”

“Right, now for the money bit. We are going to give you two thousand credits to tide you over until you start getting your own credits in a couple of weeks time.”

“Err, I don’t have a bank account.”

“You do. You get it when you get the implant. They are part of the ID thing.”

“I’m going to have to get a job, aren’t I?”

“You have one remember. Your first gig is in twelve days time.”

“Oh, yes. Sorry, I keep forgetting. There is so much happening and all at once.”

“OK, now this bit is very important. When you do a financial transaction the colour of the amount is very important. If the sum is green, you are receiving it. If it is red, you are paying them.”

“Right, so green is plus and red is minus.”

“Yes, and after each transaction your balance will pop up in your head.” added Carina.

“Right, let me send you some credits.” said Datch.

Moments later a box appeared in Kristina’s mind. It had Datch’s name on it and two thousand credits in green characters. Underneath was a box saying accept. She thought the word ‘accept’ and another box appeared saying transaction complete current balance two thousand credits.

"Oh, so I now have money?"

"Yes, two thousand credits. It should let you go shopping with Carina for clothes and anything else you might want. The vid com is linked to your implant so you can buy things using it and they get delivered to your selected location."

"Err, location. I don't know where this is other than the barn conversion."

"Oh, good point. One sec."

Datch pressed some buttons on his vid com.

"We're at location 345.355 by 453.112 plot 2. If you type that into your vid com and mark it as home, everything should come here."

"What happens if I want it to go somewhere else?"

"You can either tell it the address of the place or use current location."

"Cool."

"Right, now the work bit. I'm going to send you some files to your vid com, they are vids of our songs. Just remember you only need to learn the choruses, ok?"

"Yes."

"Right, I'm going to head over to see Mum and Dad now to sort out the weekend. I'll be back in a bit."

"OK, I'll show Kristina a bit more about the vid com." said Carina.

Datch got up and left the girls on their own.

The next few days were spent with Kristina learning the songs or at least the bits she needed to know. This involved

her singing as she walked about. Datch and Carina took time
to teach Kristina about her implant and her vid com. There
was also a lot of sorting out of the joining presents and a lot
of moving furniture about to fit things in. Datch's dad came
and helped with the barbeque adjustments so the kabab
machine could be fitted in.

The Beginning or the End.

The weekend arrived and the rest of The Pack arrived and slowly gravitated to the pool side and bar. Jep was the last to arrive and went into the bar looking stressed. Datch followed him in.

"Jep, are you ok?"

"Yes and no. Look can we get a drink and sit down over there and have a chat."

"Sure."

Datch knew something was really wrong. He poured them both a drink and they headed over to one of the sofas and sat down.

"So, what's up?"

"Ok, well, you know how I have been writing the book about us and I have a deal for it."

"Yes, it sounds like it could be a best seller."

"Well, A vid channel has asked me to host a show now as well. It's a really great deal but will mean staying on Bellatrix."

"Oh, I see."

"I don't want to leave you guys as you are family to me but I'm the oldest member of the Pack and the Arcaneus thing caused me to think about life. After seeing all that death and destruction, I started to think about where my life is going. I suppose what I'm trying to say is that I don't want to go flying around the galaxy anymore."

Datch realised that Jep was planning to leave them.

"You want to leave The Pack?" he asked.

"Yes, I suppose I do. It's been great fun but I want to stay on this planet now."

"So, when are you thinking of leaving?"

"Well, it looks like the vid deal will go through in about a month and then the first show should broadcast a few weeks after that."

"Oh. Does anyone else know?"

"No, no. I wanted to talk to you first."

"Thanks, I appreciate that. So, what do you want to do?"

"Well, I'm not sure but you've got Kristina now so it will keep things balanced. So, I would think the sooner the better, no point in dragging things out. But at the same time, I don't want to let you guys down though."

"Look, you help Kristina get ready this weekend and if you're ok with it, we could make the Barbers Inn a farewell gig for you and a welcome one for her. How about that?"

"Hmm. Ok. that's good. It will give me a few weeks to sort things out with the vid station. Can you understand my reasons for going?"

"Yes, I hear what you're saying. Do you want to tell the guys now?"

"Do you think they will be ok?"

"Yes, I'm sure they will be fine with it. Look, Let's go out together and I'll make the announcement. That way they should be fine. You're sure you want to do this?"

"Yes, it's been a really hard decision but, I'm sure."

"Ok. Let's go."

They stood up and picked up their drinks. Datch was sad but knew that Jep needed to follow his own way now. Life is not just one path but multiples of them that twisted their way through the fabric of creation and this was Jep's time to turn another corner.

They walked out onto the patio next to the pool. The guys were sitting around talking and the girls had grouped together around one of the tables. Datch coughed loudly and everyone turned around.

"Folks, can you all please listen to me."

Everyone stopped what they were doing and looked at Datch.

"I have a bit of a sad announcement to make. Jep has decided to leave us. He has explained his reasons to me and I understand and agree with them. He will be helping Kristina this weekend and then we have decided that the gig at the Barbers will be his last. I wish him well with his chosen path as I'm sure you will. He will always be part of The Pack even though he won't be with us anymore and I'm sure our paths will cross again from time to time."

Tank stood up and started to clap, one by one they all stood up and joined the clapping. Jep raised his hands.

"Thanks folks. I didn't know how to tell you. You're like family to me but I have a vid show as well as the book deal so I need to focus on that now. I will miss every one of you guys and…" he was fighting back the tears. "Well, I love you all. But… I need to make my own way now."

Datch looked at the rest of them, they all looked upset. He was. After all Jep was part of the family but what would be, would be. He cleared his throat.

"Ok, folks, let's get into party mode and celebrate Kristina joining the family and Jep's new career. We are The Pack and what we do is party."

They came over to Jep and everyone wanted to find out what he was doing. It turned out he was going to be doing a late-night chat show with various celebrity guests and Fred volunteered The Pack to be one of his guests although he did say that he would have to run it by the station first.

The party entered into music mode and the karaoke machine was turned on. Kristina got up and showed them what she could do. It impressed the girls so much that they all did a song with her, each of them taking turns to sing. The guys not to be out done did their own version.

Then there was a short break for food that was followed by a boys vs girls competition with them all taking turns singing. That carried on until late before the party entered a more chilled out phase with people sitting on the sofas chatting.

Datch sat down next to Kristina who was chatting to Carina.

"So, what do you think?" he asked.

"Think?"

"Yes, could you do this type of thing a lot?"

"Err, yes but doesn't it cause health issues?"

"Nanobots, remember nanobots. Talking of which I've put a packet of pills next to your bed. Take one before you go sleep and you won't have a hangover."

"What no hangover? oh, wow. Thanks."

"So, you can handle the fun. The stress bit comes in eight days when you do your first gig."

"Is it that bad?"

"It's not bad as such but just stressful. Well, the running onto stage bit anyway, but once the songs start, we get lost in the music and then it's party time."

"Oh, ok. I'll try to do that."

At that point Tansya came over and sat down.

"Hi Mum."

"Hi Datch. Just thought I'd come see Kristina. I haven't really had chance to talk to her since you brought her here."

"Yes, we have sort of kept her busy."

"So, Kristina how are you finding life on Bellatrix?"

"It's ok, Datch and Carina are really looking after me, but I still miss my mum a lot."

"Well, if you like and it helps you can call me mum. You've had a rough time and suffered a great loss so, if you want to talk, you can aways come to me. I have had a few thousand years of experience. ok?" she smiled at her.

"Thank you. Could you come shopping with us?"

She looked at Carina.

"Yes, it would be cool. We're going after the weekend. We need to get her a full wardrobe." said Carina.

"I don't have that much at the moment."

"Well, let's set off early and make a day of it. We can call into that restaurant at the north end of the mall for lunch. What do you think?"

Kristina looked at Carina and she nodded.

"Ok then, it's a deal."

"I'll get Dechow to pick us up in the truck to bring us home."

"How are you feeling about taking Jep's spot?"

"A bit nervous to be honest."

"Well, after watching you on the karaoke you don't need be. Just do what the rest of them do and have fun."

"I'll try. Thanks mum." she said with a grin.

Tansya smiled back.

"Ok, I'm going to watch the moons rise with Dechow so see you in a bit." said Tansya getting up.

"Thanks again."

"No problem."

Tansya headed out to Dechow who was on the old veranda looking out over the dessert. He was sitting on one of the sofas when she came out with her drink. She sat down next to him.

"How's it going in there?" he asked not taking his eyes off of the view.

"Ok, I think it's going ok. Jep's chatting to the bikers about his new career, the younger ones are playing cards except for Datch, Carina and Kristina who are chatting on the sofa. It's starting to quieten down."

"That's good. I was a bit worried things might go a bit bad when Jep said he was leaving. I think he's been a grounding force in the group. I don't know what will happen now."

"Well, after the weekend I'm going shopping with Carina and Kristina to get Kristina a new wardrobe. She needs just about everything, so I've told them you will pick us up afterwards."

"Oh. ok. Is it going to cost me?"

Tansya laughed.

"No. Just your time."

"I suppose it will give me and Datch time to start the extension he's asked for."

"Well, they do need more space now that there are three of them."

"It's not for them. It's for the holo vid system the President got them as a joining present. It needs a very large room to allow it to work correctly. So, we're expanding out from the side of the lounge."

"Oh! good luck with that."

"I think we're going to need it."

"Oh, look a shooting star."

Dechow looked at his watch.

"No, just the eleven o'clock shuttle from the space station."

They both laughed.

The next morning The Pack retired to the barn near Datch and Carina's house. One of the barns was now their house but the other was still a normal barn. The Pack had made the stable section of it into a studio of sorts. It didn't have the studio equipment like the one at Tank's but it did have some sofas, a fridge with cold drinks in and plenty of space to set up their instruments. They sat listening to a recording of some Earth music that Datch had told the ship to record while they were there. Kristina was feeling really good about being able to explain about the songs that she had grown up with on

Earth. Datch sat taking the songs apart and then working out if they could use some of the bits.

It was slow going at first with nothing but a number of song ideas. Then piece by piece a song started to take shape.

It was about the slavery of a planet and then finished with the battle for freedom. Of course, it was a rock number and had an underlying repeating riff that Datch had found in one of the said Earth songs. They called it 'Freedom'. After they had got the basics sorted out, they went through some of their songs with Kristina.

They focused on her bits and were pleasantly impressed with how fast she was picking it up. They all decided that she would be fine on stage at the Barbers, she wasn't so sure but Jep was coaching her and told her that he didn't know half the songs when he started so he just copied Tank. He also told her to look out for flying underwear. She looked at him gone out when he said it until Fred told the story about the woman who had a crush on Tank. They had ended up meeting her by accident one night in the Barbers and Fred had to explain to her that Tank wasn't currently interested in the female gender and was looking for a man. She still insisted on giving him a kiss on the cheek though and telling him if he ever changed his mind to look her up. This stopped most of the flying underwear but a piece would turn up every few months as a gentle reminder. However, they were normally new ones and on a couple of occasions came still in the packaging.

During the practice session they found out that if they dropped the male voices a bit and boosted Kristina's they could cause the voices to harmonise an octave higher making Green Gem, Black Spiders Die and Supernova sound even better.

They carried on until the sun was going down and then went to the bar for some food that Tansya had made for them. The stars came out and two of the moons slowly climbed up the star-studded blackness into the sky above the dessert. The insects came out and were making a soft chirping noise. The evening was spent chilling on the veranda and playing darts in the bar.

The next day was the same, they spent the morning working on the new song and then the first part of the afternoon was handed over to the girls who had got a song they wanted to try. They called it 'Girl Power' and this time all four of them were on the mics. The drum kit was on automatic so Tish could take front of stage. They did it four times and decided it was a good song but would need a bit more refining for it to work. They put a target date of three months to get it ready to perform along with 'Freedom'.

Afterwards it was practice time for Kristina, this time she had to do the chorus with just Fred. This was so they could hear her better. This just confirmed to them that she was ready. They went through all of their songs and there was only one that she struggled with and Jep was there again helping her out and encouraging her.

The evening was again a chilled out one in the bar except for the younger members of The Pack who had a two-hour session of Solar Ball in the Raven's cargo bay.

The next morning a load of supplies turned up from the building supplies company in the city. They were the parts for Datch's extension which both him and his dad were going to make a start on while the girls were in the city shopping. It would give them time to get the foundation down and maybe the walls up before Dechow had to fetch them.

The morning was again spent working on the new songs and a bit more practice for Kristina which led up to lunch time when it was decided that they had done enough for now and an afternoon around the pool was called for.

Everyone got into their swim wear as sessions around the pool could quite easily involve getting wet even if you weren't planning to enter the pool. Water wars would sporadically break out and water would go everywhere. Datch would normally start it by chasing Carina and this afternoon was no different.

Datch got out to have a drink and while he was gone Carina nicked the inflatable chair that he had been floating in. When he came back to the pool, he retaliated by diving in at the deep end and swimming up underneath her and capsizing the chair with her in it. She then grabbed the end of the inflatable banana to stop herself going under. This was very unfortunate for Hagger who was sitting on it at the time and was catapulted into the water with a big splash that drowned Dapo, Tish, Rosey and Kristina.

The pool then became the site of a full-scale water battle. The bikers had seen it coming and covered the tops of their glasses with beermats to stop their beer getting diluted. Jep on the other hand had been inside getting another drink when it started and just happened to walk outside at the wrong time. He was then hit by a full salvo from Hagger and Dapo. He looked at them and then at his glass that was now dripping wet and had more liquid in than it did moments before. He shrugged his shoulders and carried on walking over to the bikers table taking a course that took him out of range of most of the flying water.

The conflict carried on for half an hour before it started to calm down into a few minor skirmishes. By the time Dechow and Tansya came out, the warring parties had agreed upon a truce and were laying on the sunbeds having a drink.

"Who wants some food?" asked Dechow.

There was a general agreement that food would be good. Dechow started a barbeque and Tansya fetched out some salad and rolls that she had already prepared inside.

She sat down next to Fred. After they had been chatting for a few moments Tansya asked,

"So, do you think Kristina will fit in?"

Fred looked at Kristina for a moment. She was sitting with Rosey and Carina eating her burger.

"She seems like a nice person and she has quite a voice on her. A bit of the Datch magic and I think she'll be fine."

"Do you think she'll cope with The Pack's habit of getting into err, spots?"

"You mean trouble. Well, by the sound of it, she's already done that with Datch and Carina, so I can't see a problem there. She's a good kid I think and we get good vibes off her."

"Yes, she does seem like a nice person."

They sat back eating their food watching the others. The afternoon turned into evening and finally night.

They were sitting on the veranda when Datch came back from his house carrying a box.

Clax nudged Tank,

"I bet I know what's in that box." He said.

"What?" Asked Tank.

"Well, it's going to be black and green with writing on the back."

"Oh." he said as realised what it was.

Datch walked up the steps onto the balcony and placed the box on a small table.

"Kristina. Please can you come here." He said looking at her.

She got up and walked over to him.

"Kristina, we have all agreed that you are now to be one of The Pack. So, it is my duty as leader of The Pack to give you your robes of office."

"My robes of office?"

"Yes, we have a certain look on stage and as you are now one of us you sort of need to wear it. Either that or Tish and Rosey will get very cross with you."

They all laughed.

"Anyway, please except your T-shirt and skirt."

He handed them to her.

"Thank you."

"Now for your accessories. Your official dark glasses and baseball cap."

The glasses were a premium brand and baseball cap was of course black in colour."

"And last but most important the Jacket."

He got a black leather jacket out of the box. It had the green flames, Her name on the Lapel and 'The Pack On Tour' in big green letters on the back with 'Free Beer Welcome' in small red letters underneath.

"Oh wow. Thanks."

"Go on then. Put it on." Shouted Tish.

Kristina put the jacket on.

"Now you look the part." Said Carina.

Kristina turned around showing off the jacket.

"Put the rest on." Said Peebop.

"Ok, back in a minute."

She went off to one of the spare rooms and got changed. Five minutes later she came back with the rest on. Datch looked her up and down as she turned around in front of him.

"Now you look like one of us." he said.

The others all cheered and then started telling her how good she looked in it.

The next morning everyone was up early. The bikers had offered to help Datch and his dad with the extension and Rosey, Tish and Dapo had offered to take Carina, Kristina and Tansya into the city with Hagger following behind. This saved the girls getting a taxi.

Jep was late coming down to breakfast, the girls were just leaving as he arrived downstairs. He said his goodbyes to them and then went over to Datch.

"Hi Datch, I've been doing some thinking and decided it might be a good idea to get my stuff from the Raven while I'm here."

"Oh. are you sure?" Datch was hoping he would change his mind.

"Yes, or I'll only have to come back at some point and that would make me feel awkward."

"I see what you mean. Well, grab a coffee and go and do it. Come and find me afterwards, ok?"

"Ok."

Datch left Jep to go off to get a coffee and something to eat. He headed outside to the work crew that was assembling outside of his house.

"Well folks. Time to get stuck in." he said walking up to them.

They started to get the foundation laid out for the new room. It was quite large as it needed to be big enough for the holo vid system and also a Solar Ball system that was also being added. Datch had figured that as the holo emitters were there he may as well add a Solar Ball console to it.

The bots were just laying the base down when Jep came walking over looking a bit down in the dumps.

"Hey dude, you, ok?" asked Tank.

"Yes Tank. I'm ok. Datch, I've done it. I'll see you all at the Barbers for the gig."

"Ok Jep. See you there and don't be late."

"No, I won't. I don't want to miss my own send off." he smiled.

He turned to head back to his bike.

"See you dudes!" he shouted as he went.

Tank turned to Datch.

"What did he mean, it's done?" he asked.

"He wanted to take his stuff from the Raven so he didn't have to come back and do it later."

"Oh. I see." said Tank looking down.

"Hey, we're all feeling the same about it. But it's his life and he needs to follow his own path. At the end of the day, he will always be part of our family."

"Yes. I know dude."

"We'll still see him at the Barbers, and he will be able to buy the beers on expenses now."

"He does anyway the same as me." Said Clax who had been helping Jep do his taxes.

"He does?" Said Fred.

"Yes. All the ones on this planet anyway."

"Oh. You'll have to show me how to do that later on."

"No probs, dude."

"Right, let's get this done before the girls come back." said Datch

In the city, Tish and Rosey had decided to help Kristina shop for clothes as well, stating that they were fashion experts of a kind. They sent the boys home before descending on the shopping mall like a pack of hungry vultures. They set themselves a goal of going through every clothes shop on the left side by lunch time and then they were going to do the right-hand side in the afternoon.

Kristina was amazed by the selection of styles and also the number of arms and legs some of them had. They ended up buying three large rucksacks to put all the clothes and shoes in and took it in turns to stand outside the shops with them. The girls were a big help to Kristina, helping her to get items that were in fashion and easy to wear. There were new fabrics for her to try the feel of, not to mention the countless accessories that the shops had.

They found lots of tops, skirts, shorts and a few dresses that she liked. On Earth she had a few clothes but they were lost when the drug lord's men had burnt their village down.

This was a fresh start for her. It was like winning the lottery a thousand times over and every minute there was something new, whether it be an alien walking past them, some strange creation in a shop or a robot flying overhead. This new world was an incredible place.

When they said they were going shopping for a new wardrobe for her they meant it. And apparently, it was coming tomorrow.

They slowly made their way towards the food section at the far end. The smells from the different types of food were getting stronger as they approached.

They arrived at the food court just as lunch time rush was starting. The food court was a large circular area with restaurants around the outside and tables and chairs in the centre which had small stalls dotted about in amongst them.

The area contained the smells of a thousand worlds, all of which bombarded your nostrils with a mish mash of scents and flavours. Some of them didn't smell very nice while others made your mouth start watering almost instantly. Strange fruits and meats were hanging down from some for the stalls and a large number of aliens were sitting down eating some very odd-looking dishes.

"So, everyone good with the Orion Star?" asked Tansya.

Everyone agreed it was a good plan especially as the less expensive places were starting to get very full. They headed over to a restaurant at the far side of the food court. It had 'Orion Star' in big golden letters above the door and there was a sign saying please wait to be seated next to the door. They waited and a waiter came over and escorted them to a table.

"So, what we having?" asked Tansya.

"Err, I don't know what any of this is." said Kristina.

"Don't forget, you can use your implant." Carina reminded her in a kind way.

"Oh. Yes." she said and started to study the menu.

"What does Jacor taste like?" she asked.

"Err, sort of lemony." Said Rosey.

"So, lemony chicken. Sorry, I mean Hacks."

"Yes, you normally get a side order of err rice with that."

"Hmm, I think I'll go with that then."

They all decided what they were going to have and ordered it.

"Can I ask something?" said Kristina as the food turned up.

"What?"

"Well, people seem to all be happy. I don't think I've seen one sad person since I've been here. Is life that good here?"

"People do get sad here, just not very much. They have jobs with flexible hours and because the factories are fully automated most of them work from home. If you don't have an income the government will find you a job." said Tansya.

"We did have a lot of homeless people but they all got eaten." added Tish who was trying to eat a large sausage thing and still look lady like.

"They got eaten?" said Kristina looking alarmed.

"Yes, we had an arachnoid problem. Datch and Dechow killed it in the end." said Carina.

"Datch did?"

"Yes, it was sort of payback for killing him." said Rosey.

"Oh. So, he died?"

"Most of him did. His brain was transported aboard the Carpaycus and he got a new body." said Tish.

"It scared me senseless." added Carina.

Kristina thought for a moment.

"Was that what you meant on Earth when you said you thought you had lost someone?"

"Yes. But let's not talk about that."

"Oh. ok, so why did it eat the homeless?"

"They were an easy target, not traceable and no one would miss them."

"How big was it?"

"About the size of two Jaxx." Say Rosey.

"Are there any more out there?"

"No, not on this world and their world is on the far side of the galaxy."

She relaxed again.

"So, there were homeless?"

"Yes, but they were like that by choice. They refused the implant and because of that were pretty much unemployable and they couldn't even be given a home as all the locking systems connect to your implant to lock and unlock the doors."

"Oh, so the implant is that important?"

"Yes, you will soon wonder how you ever lived without it." said Tish.

"So, did you have any boy or girlfriends on Earth?" asked Rosey.

"I had a couple in the city when I was at school but nothing serious. I was too busy with school work."

"School work?" asked Tish.

"Yes, on Earth we had to learn maths, science, history and languages. We would have to do homework to make sure we had understood what we had been shown in class."

"Oh wow. Not social skills then?"

"Not as such, but we sort of worked them out for ourselves in the playgrounds."

"Playgrounds? Are they some form of night clubs?" asked Rosey.

Kristina laughed.

"No, they are the area outside the school but still within the school grounds. We would get a break in the morning and one at lunch time. Me and my friends would play games and as we got older we would sit looking at the boys and marking them out of ten."

"I think we've all done that one." said Carina.

"And what did Datch score?"

"About a twelve."

They all laughed.

They finished their food and drinks off and then set about the second assault on the mall.

Shop by shop, they slowly worked their way back down the opposite side of the mall. As they went, it wasn't just Kristina who was buying things, all of them were now carrying

bags with things they had spotted. A number of fans spotted
Carina, Rosey and Tish and wanted pictures with them.
Kristina watched as they posed with them and signed some
bits of paper. After they had gone, she turned to them.

"Does that happen a lot?"

"Remember the dark glasses and baseball cap. That's
what they are for. They hide us from the public and makes
them unsure if it's us or not. We forgot to put them on today."

"Oh, so don't forget my shades. Noted."

"Shades?"

"Yes, we called them shades in the city on Earth."

"Oh, cool, shades it is then. That sounds much better than
dark glasses." Said Rosey

They finally arrived at the end of the mall heavily loaded
up with bags. Tansya fetched out her vid com and called
Dechow.

Dechow was sitting with Datch and the bikers having a
beer and admiring their workmanship or more to the point the
bot's automaton skills as it was the bots that had done most
of the heavy work. They had managed to get the building up
and the roof on, thanks to the bikers help. Ok, the insides
were missing but at least the structure was complete. Datch
and Dechow could quite easily finish off the remaining bits at
their leisure. They were just debating the best colour to make
the inside when Dechow's vid com started playing a tune. He
fetched it out and looked at it.

"It's your mum." He said and pressed the answer button.

"Hi Tansya."

There was a sort pause.

"OK, no probs, on my way."

He put his vid in his pocket.

"Ok, I'm going to fetch the girls. If you guys want to hang about, I'm going to get a barbeque started when I come back."

"Sounds good." Said Clax.

"OK, but I can't stop too late. I have a hair appointment at ten in the morning." Said Tank.

"I thought you had stopped doing that?" said Fred.

"I have, I need a perm."

"Oh."

Peebop and Clax just nodded.

"Ok. I'll see you in a bit." Said Dechow and went off to get in his truck.

The next few days were spent with Datch and Dechow finishing off the extension and Carina going through the set lists with Kristina so that she was confident about all of the songs. The day of the gig arrived.

Show Time

The morning was bright and sunny. The weather service had been watering the landscape overnight and the ground was still damp from the rain that came at five in the morning and stopped at six.

It was mid-morning by the time Datch and Carina got up. Kristina was already outside sitting on the patio having her breakfast and enjoying the sunshine. They went outside and sat having a coffee with her.

"So, what's the plan for today?" Kristina asked.

"We'll head into the city around three-ish this afternoon and have a drink, then we dump our bags in our room's just before the gig. You have the small single room at the back. It's a bit small but you're only sleeping there."

"How come we're not coming back here?"

"We like to chill out after the gig and normally we'll go to the pancake shop in the morning."

"Yeh, we have a routine at the Barbers, it's something we have done ever since school."

"Ok, I like pancakes." Said Kristina.

"They do nice cookies as well. The double chocolate chip ones are to die for."

"I think I'll get some of them to bring home with us tomorrow."

Carina looked at her and smiled, it was the first time she had called their house home.

"Good idea, we can have some to go with our lunch later on."

They finished their breakfast and Carina and Kristina went inside to watch the vid. Datch went into the new extension to try and get the Solar Ball system to talk to the holo emitters. He had the feeling that the Solar Ball system was being told to share them with the new holo vid system and didn't like it because it wanted to have them all to itself.

The afternoon arrived and they had some lunch followed by a shower and then they packed their rucksacks with overnight stuff. Datch and Carina collected their instruments and placed them on the racks attached to the bikes. Tansya came over and wished Kristina good luck and then watched them get on the bikes and fly off in the direction of the city.

The Barbers Inn was very busy when they arrived. Jim was doing a great trade in food and there were quite a lot of chocolate sundaes being sold, word had got around about them and everyone wanted one.

Datch, Carina and Kristina walked in through the doors and nodded at Jim. Carina and Kristina headed up the stairs while Datch took their instruments over to the stage and placed them at the back.

They were the first to arrive and sat down at the big table with their bags next to them.

"When do we put the bags in our rooms?"

"We normally do it before we head to our dressing room. That way we can get changed in our rooms before coming down."

"That sounds good."

Jim came up the stairs carrying a tray of drinks.

"Hi folks." He said walking up to the table.

"Hi Jim. How's it going?"

"Good Thanks Datch. You?"

"Ok thanks but I have some bad news and some good news." Said Datch.

Jim stopped what he was doing and looked at him.

"Err, Bad news?"

"Yes, and good."

"Oh, go on then."

"First the bad news. Jep is leaving The Pack to become a chat show host."

"Oh wow. What's made him do that?"

"Well, He says he's too old for being shot at and chased across the galaxy. Also, the vid company made him a very good offer."

"Ok, so what's the good news?"

"Kristina is going to replace him."

"Well, welcome aboard." said Jim looking at Kristina.

"Thanks."

"So, tonight they will both be on stage so if you can sort the credits so Kristina gets her share as well. It is also going to be Jep's last gig so we're going to try and give him a good send off."

"Ok, I can sort the credits out. I'll fetch the terminal in a minute so I can register her ID with it. Do you want me to do anything different?"

"No, I'll do the announcement when I get on stage."

"OK, no problem. I'll just go and fetch the terminal. Just a thought but have you let Joni know?"

"No, to be honest we have been so busy I never thought about it. I'll give him a call."

"Ok, I'll be right back."

Jim headed off downstairs and Datch got out his vid com to call Joni.

"Who is Joni?" Kristina asked Carina.

"He's the host of the biggest music show on the planet and also a good friend. He was the one who helped us get to where we are now."

"Oh. So, he's a big celebrity?"

"Yes, but so are we and just remember, after tonight you will be too."

"I never thought of it like that."

Jim came back up the stairs holding a small hand scanner.

"OK Kristina, just accept the transaction, it will be for one credit. Then the system can store your details for later."

He pressed a button on the terminal and a box appeared in her mind asking her if she wished to accept the transaction. She accepted it and another box appeared showing 1 credit in green. The terminal beeped, he pressed another couple of buttons and it beeped again.

"There you go, all done. Right, I'll see you all later."

"Thanks."

Jim headed off down the stairs.

Datch finished his call with Joni and put his vid com on the table.

"What did he say?" Asked Carina.

"He's going to send a vid crew down as he doesn't want to miss Jep's last gig and Kristina's first."

"You mean we're going to be on TV?" Kristina was now starting to look nervous.

"Yes, but it's being recorded not live." Said Datch trying to make it sound better.

This didn't seem to help much.

"Look, the vid bots are so small you won't even see them, just remember the songs and focus on the music. We're all up there together as one. You are part of The Pack on stage, not an individual. So, don't worry. You have us all alongside you."

"I'm a bit nervous now."

"We all get a bit nervous before a gig. But when the music starts you forget about all the people and sing to each other. That works really well for me. Datch is the showman, He works the crowd." said Carina.

"I do?"

"Yes, you play them like your guitar."

"Oh, I never realised it. I just have fun with them."

Just then a very big shadow fell over Datch.

Kristina looked up and up and then found a face.

"Hi Timbo." said Datch.

"Hi Datch, Hi Carina. Did you have a nice honeymoon?"

"Yes, thanks Timbo." said Carina.

"Timbo, this is Kristina. She is going to be singing backing vocals for us from now on."

"Hello Kristina. Welcome to The Pack."

"Thank you."

"Also, Timbo. I have some bad news; Jep is going to be leaving us after tonight."

"Oh. Why?"

"He's got a job as a vid channel chat show host and wants to stay on Bellatrix. Anyway, we're going to try and make this a good send off for him."

"Ok. Can I do anything to help?"

Datch thought for a moment.

"You know that drink he likes, see if you can get a bottle of it."

"Ok Datch, I'll sort it. What sort of drink do you have, Kristina?"

"Err, I have beer, why?"

"I get the drinks ready for the break so that they are waiting for you when you come off the stage."

"Oh. cool."

"Datch, I'll go and start setting up."

"Ok Timbo."

The shadow that was over Datch left and headed for the stairs.

"Wow, he's big." Said Kristina after he had gone.

"Yes, he manages all of our needs." said Carina.

"I can see what you meant about him. He could get hit by a bus and the bus would lose."

"Yes, Timbo is an unstoppable force but at the same time he is a gentle giant." said Datch.

"I don't know what we would do without him." added Carina.

Just then Hagger came walking up the stairs with Rosey.

One by one the rest of The Pack assembled.

The afternoon turned into evening and after a light meal Carina turned to them all.

"I suppose we had better go and get ready." she said.

They all agreed and headed to their rooms to get changed.

Kristina laid her t-shirt and skirt on the bed and looked at them for a few moments. She took her clothes off and put them on. It felt strange but in a good way. She looked at herself in the mirror and smiled.

Thirty minutes later they headed back down the stairs and Carina showed Kristina the back way to the dressing room. An extra chair had been added to the large table in the centre of the room and a round of drinks had been placed on the table in their normal seating position ready for them. They all filed in and sat down.

"So, are we doing the normal set list?" asked Fred.

"Yes, but I want to try to get the harmonies going like we did in the barn. So, try and get them to resonate, ok?"

"Ok."

After they had gone through the set list Datch had a quick look through the stage door. The bar was getting packed and people were still coming in through the doors. Up on the balcony he could see the vid bot operators. He shut the door and went back to the table.

"It's a full house folks." he said sitting down.

"Is Joni's crew in?" asked Peebop.

"Yes, two of them on the balcony."

"I'm getting very nervous folks." said Kristina.

"It will be fine. Just follow our lead and don't forget to smile." said Carina.

"So, I take it Joni is giving us the normal fee?" asked Fred.

"Yes, he is."

"Fee?" asked Kristina.

"Yes, he pays us twenty thousand credits for the gig which is about seventeen hundred a piece."

"Cool, I'll be able to go shopping again."

"We could make a day of it next time, if you like?" asked Rosey who had enjoyed someone new to shop with.

"Yes, that would be good."

"OK, but this time let's get the stuff delivered home." said Carina realising the thought of it was distracting Kristina and calming her nerves.

"We could go to Castor's for lunch." said Rosey.

"Yes. Shall we make it just the four of us this time?" asked Tish.

"Ok." said Carina. "What about next week, the day after we get back from the gig in the capital?"

"Sounds good to me." said Rosey.

"Me too." said Tish.

"Cool. It's a date." Said Kristina.

The door opened and Jim walked in.

"You about ready folks?" he asked.

"Yes." said Datch and stood up.

Jim went back out the door and onto the stage to announce them.

Datch put his hand out and one by one they put their hands on top of his. Kristina looked at them and put her hand on the top.

"One, two, three. Let's party!"

They all let go and headed for the door. Jep grabbed Kristina's hand and led her out on stage.

The bar was rammed full of people and they were all cheering at them. Kristina's heart started to race as she stepped up to the mic next to Tank and Jep.

"Hello Barbers." yelled Datch into his mic.

A big cheer erupted from the bar.

"This is a very special night folks. Tonight. Sadly, Jep is leaving us to move on to pastures new. But watch out for his new chat show coming soon."

He paused and there was a loud cheer from the crowd.

"Also, I would like you all to give a warm welcome to our new member Kristina who will be taking Jep's place!"

There was another huge roar from the crowd.

"OK. Are you ready to Party?"

They all screamed at the stage.

Datch turned and nodded at Tish.

The music blasted out and then the gems energised. Kristina felt the music take hold of her and as all the gems energies combined, she lost sight of the crowd in a green haze. The music flooded through her soul like a tsunami of sound and rhythm. She sang her heart out and with every note felt more a part of the music. It reached the end of the first set and they all ran off stage.

They sat around the table trying to cool down. After they had a good drink of beer, Carina turned to Kristina.

"How are your nerves now?"

"Err, I think I lost them somewhere on the stage." She was looking at the sparkles cascading off of her head like a water fall of green light.

The rest of The Pack were looking like they had been sitting too close to a nuclear reactor.

They cooled off and then it was time for the second set. They bounced onto the stage and straight into the first song. The bar was full of big smiles and lots of people sparkling. They were all singing along with the songs and at the end of the last song when the cheers had died down a bit Datch said.

"I would like you all to put your hands together for Jep."

A spot light lit Jep up although he didn't need any lighting up. He waved and there was a big cheer.

"Now please give Kristina a cheer."

The spotlight turned to Kristina. She waved and there was another big cheer.

"Ok, One more song folks. Supernova."

The music blasted out and the room erupted.

They ended up doing two more songs before finally leaving the stage.

They were all towers of green light when they left the stage. They went and sat in the dressing room chilling out.

"Timbo, do you have the item I asked you for?" asked Datch.

"Yes, here you go Datch."

He passed him a bottle and Datch stood up and looked at Jep.

"Jep, I know this is not good bye as such as we'll be still seeing you in the Barbers or around at Tanks but I thought we should give you something for your support over the last few years. So, please accept this as a token of our thanks. You will always be welcome to join us whenever we're about."

He passed him the bottle. Jep looked at it and then cleared his throat.

"Thank you Datch, Thanks all of you. It's been a lot of fun over the last few years and we've had a fair few scrapes as well. What with fighting spiders, saving planets and not to forget the parties. I will miss it all and I think part of me will always want to be with you. I love you guys and well, thanks for the ride."

The rest of them clapped.

"Well, here is to your new path in life, I hope you find what you're looking for." said Datch lifting his glass.

They all lifted their glasses.

"Cheers!" they all said.

They all took a drink.

Jep looked thoughtful for a moment before turning to Kristina.

"Kristina, I want you to know these folks around this table are some of the best people in the galaxy. You have been given the chance to be part of the magic that is The Pack. Hold on tight and enjoy every bit of the ride."

"Yes, Kristina you are now part of the family." Said Fred.

Datch lifted his glass again.

"To The Pack!" he said.

They all repeated 'The Pack' and took a drink.

"Ok, let's see if it's safe to head to the big table. Timbo."

Timbo looked out the door. The crowd had thinned out and it looked safe-ish to go upstairs. He signalled to Jim who sent a couple of bouncers over to escort them along behind the bar and up to the big table on the balcony.

The next two days went past and the weekend approached. They had decided to take the Raven to the capital after all and leave it at a VIP area near the centre as they couldn't be bothered to spend eight hours on an intercontinental shuttle. The Raven would complete the trip in an hour and that was allowing for heavy traffic.

It was mid-morning when people started to turn up. Datch took Kristina inside the Raven.

They walked in through the cargo bay and into the ship Datch walked along the corridor and stopped at a door. It had a small plaque on it saying Kristina.

"This is your own room. If you wish to change the insides, you can. Just ask me and we can change the colours and carpets to whatever you wish. Bedding, towels and cuddly toys, I'll leave to you."

"Thanks."

"Now come over to this terminal please."

They walked down the corridor a bit to a terminal on the wall.

"Computer, Please add Kristina to the ships crew."

"Kristina please state your name." said the computer.

"My name is Kristina Martínez."

"Welcome aboard Kristina."

"Does this mean the Raven will give me food when I want it?"

"Yes, you'll be able to do just about everything apart from fly her."

"Cool."

"Ok. Go get your bits, we'll be going soon."

They went outside and The Pack started loading their stuff on board.

Lunch time approached and The Pack headed to the cockpit.

They sat down. Kristina was now sitting next to Fred as that had been Jep's seat.

"Everyone ready?"

They all nodded.

"Yuland city control, this is the Raven requesting a low orbital course to the Capital."

"Good morning, Raven. Traffic currently heavy. Lock on to beacon 1023KTY112 and launch in 30 seconds. Automatic flight is available."

"Yuland City. Locking on to beacon and requesting auto."

"Autopilot will activate on lift off."

Datch brought the thrusters online and the Raven lifted off the ground.

"Yuland City, Raven is yours."

Moments later the Raven carried The Pack into the sky and the new future that lay ahead of them.

The End

Other Books in the Chronicles of Datch Series.

Datch – The Great Adventure.

The Datch Pack.

The Mystical Gem.

Arcaneus.

Hunting Jackars.

The Orphaned World.